tunneling to the
center of the earth

D1020991

tunneling to the center of the earth

: stories **:**

kevin wilson

AN ecco BOOK

HARPER PERENNIAL

NEW YORK • LONDON • TORONTO • SYDNEY • NEW DELHI • AUCKLAND

HARPER ● PERENNIAL

Some of these stories first appeared in slightly different form in the following publications: *The Cincinnati Review* ("Grand Stand-In"), *Ploughshares* ("Blowing Up on the Spot"), *DIAGRAM* ("The Dead Sister Handbook: A Guide for Sensitive Boys"), *The Greensboro Review* ("Birds in the House"), *The Frostproof Review* and *New Stories from the South: The Year's Best, 2006* ("Tunneling to the Center of the Earth"), *Meridian* ("The Shooting Man"), *The Carolina Quarterly* and *New Stories from the South: The Year's Best, 2005* ("The Choir Director Affair"), *One Story* ("Worst-Case Scenario").

HarperCollins books may be purchased for educational, business, or sales promotional use. For information please write: Special Markets Department, HarperCollins Publishers, 10 East 53rd Street, New York, NY 10022.

FIRST EDITION

Designed by Laura Kaeppel

Library of Congress Cataloging-in-Publication Data is available upon request.

ISBN 978-0-06-157902-8

09 10 11 12 13   OV/RRD   10 9 8 7 6 5 4 3 2

For Debbie, Kelly, and Kristen Wilson, who made me.

And for Leigh Anne Couch, who keeps me.

There's nothing in this warm, vegetal dusk
That is not beautiful or that will last.

—"TROPICAL COURTYARD" BY JOE BOLTON

One hopes for so much from a chicken and is so
dreadfully disillusioned.

—"THE EGG" BY SHERWOOD ANDERSON

contents

tunneling to the
center of the earth

grand stand-in

the key to this job is to always remember that you aren't replacing anyone's grandmother. You aren't trying to be a better grandmother than the first one. For all intents and purposes, you *are* the grandmother, and always have been. And if you can do this, can provide this level of grandmotherliness with each family, every time, then you can make a good career out of this. Not to say that it isn't weird sometimes. Because it is. More often than not, actually, it is incredibly, undeniably weird.

I never had a family of my own. I didn't get married, couldn't see the use of it. Most of my own family is gone now, and the ones that are still around, I don't see anymore. To most people, I probably look like an old maid, buying for one, and this is perfectly fine with me. I like my privacy; if I go to bed with someone, it isn't a person who has to spend his entire life with me afterward. I like the dimensions of the space I take up, and I am happy. But it's not hard to imagine what it would have been like: husband, children, grandchildren, pictures on the mantle, visits at Christmas, a big funeral, and people who would inherit my money. You can be happy with your life and yet still see the point of one lived differently. That's why it seemed so natural when I saw this ad in the paper: "Grandmothers Wanted—No Experience Necessary."

I am an employee of Grand Stand-In, a Nuclear Family Supplemental Provider. It's pretty simple. With so many new families popping up, upwardly mobile couples with new children, there is a segment of this demographic, more than you would think, who no longer have any living parents. So many of these new parents feel their children are missing out on a crucial part of their life experience, grandparents. And that's where I come in.

I currently serve as a grandmother to five families in the Southeast. Each role is different, though I specialize in the single, still-active grandmother archetype, usually the paternal grandmother, husband now deceased, quite comfortable but not rich, still pretty, fond of crafts. I am fifty-six years old but I can play younger or older depending on what is needed. The families work out the rest of the details with the company. Old photos are doctored to include my image, a backstory is created, and phone calls and visits are carefully planned. For each project, we call them *fams*, I am required to memorize a family history that goes back eight generations. It's difficult work, but it's fairly lucrative, nearly ten thousand a year, per family; and with Social Security going down the tubes, it's nice to have spending money. But that alone can't keep you interested. It's hard to describe the feeling you get from opening your door, the inside of your house untouched by feet other than your own for so long, and finding a little boy or girl who is so excited to see you, has thought of little else for the past few days. You feel like a movie star, all the attention. They run into your arms and shout your name, though not your real name, and you are all that they care about.

°°

I go by Gammy, MeeMaw, Grandma Helen, Mimi, and, weirdly enough, Gammy once again. At the beginning, I had trouble responding when someone said my fam name, but you get used to it.

°°

Tonight, while I'm writing birthday, congratulations, and first communion cards for the month, all for different families, I get a call from my family arranger, with offers of new jobs. "The first is easy," he says, "just a six-week job, a not-dead-yet, one kid."

A "not-dead-yet" is when a family purchases, in weekly installments, a phone call from a grandparent who has, still unbeknownst to the child, recently died. It allows the parents time to decide what to say to the child, how to break the news to them. It's a hundred dollars a call, no face time, but it's morbid and I try to avoid them. Still, I have a fairly easy phone schedule for this upcoming month, and it's useful to practice your voice skills, so I take it.

"The next one," he says, "is a little different than usual. We need somebody with good disconnect skills, so of course I immediately thought of you."

"Face time?" I ask.

"Lots of face time," he says. "We're looking at weekly face time."

The more face time, the more preparation required. On the plus side, it makes it easier to establish a bond with the children. It pays a lot more too.

"Okay," I tell him. "I can handle it. What makes it so different? Do I have a husband?"

"No," he says, "It's not that. It's a switch job."

A switch job means the child already knows the actual grandparent but a switch is needed due to an unforeseen death. It has to be done just right, usually with situations where the family rarely sees the grandparent. A switch job with lots of face time could be a problem. You don't want to make it worse on the child, add insult to injury.

"Let me think about it," I tell him.

"Well, think about this too," he says, and then he is quiet for three, maybe four, seconds. "She's still alive."

$$\vdots\vdots$$

I am the queen of disconnect. Stand-ins must remember that fams are the client. You work for them. And yet you have to love them as if you have known them your entire life. The job requires you to spend large amounts of time not thinking about your fam, and then throwing yourself into the moment as if you haven't stopped. Stand-ins must not, under any circumstances, intrude upon the lives of their fams beyond the agreed-upon situations. You cannot surprise them with a call when you are feeling lonely. You cannot arrive at their house because you just happen to be in the area. People who actually are grandparents seem to have the most trouble with this, this belief that family is forever. For stand-ins, family is only for the moment, for a few hours, and if you are good, you do not forget this.

And I am the best. I get the highest approval ratings from my families, lots of monthly report cards that read, *I wish she really were my mother* or *Can we adopt her?*, but I don't miss them when they are gone. I love them, but I know what kind of love it is. Disconnecting may seem cold, but it is what is required. And I am, as I have been told many times, so damn good at it.

◦◦
◦◦

Later that night, I call the arranger back. "I'll take it," I say. I have lots of love to give.

◦◦
◦◦

A few days later, at the community center, I tell some of the other stand-ins about the situation. Community centers are good places for stand-ins, free classes on subjects that are necessary to be effective. Every week, I take classes on many of the so-called "granny skills" that are so prized by clients: cooking, knitting, sewing (which I am particularly bad at), and flower arranging. The more skills you have, the more jobs you get. After a few classes, you can spot the other stand-ins, taking copious notes, and now we have a book club made up only of stand-ins, though we never read and only ever talk about our fams.

"So this switch job, what's wrong with the real granny?" Martha asks. Martha specializes in multiple-husband, slightly alcoholic grandmothers who come from money. Martha does the opposite of disconnect; she works the families so well that she erases the need for disconnect, which allows her to show up, unannounced, at any of her families' houses, usually around dinner, and they will welcome her inside. She has been doing this longer than anyone else I know, and she is very good at what she does.

"I don't know," I say. "Maybe she doesn't get along with the family. She might be opting out and heading down to Florida."

"Not likely," Martha says. "Granny's don't leave. This is a family move. She's in a wheelchair, I bet, or has some kind of degenerative disease. They want someone active."

"Are you going to take it?" another woman asks.

"I already have," I say. "I don't like switches but it's good money."

"For weekly face time money," Martha says, "I'd do it and I'd even take care of their extra granny problem."

All of us laugh, no hesitation, and when we finally stop, Martha looks around at us, smiling.

"For kind old ladies," she tells us, "we are such bitches."

°°
°°

One of my fams is coming today so I start preparing. I go into my study and take out the box marked FERGUSON FAM. Inside, there are framed pictures, gifts from the grandchildren to be prominently displayed, an indexed ledger of past visits, and recipes for their favorite foods. I like the Fergusons. The two grandchildren are wonderful, bright and sensitive and affectionate. Both parents are enthusiastic about the situation, which is always best. It is hard to work with the children when one of the parents is constantly staring at you, thinking of all the things they could buy if they didn't have to retain your services.

I set up the pictures, place a few issues of *Reader's Digest* on the coffee table, and get to work on the meal, a traditional fried chicken dinner with mashed potatoes and corn on the cob, with coconut cream pie for dessert. Until this job, I'd never made a pie in my entire life. For my first fam dinner, the blueberry pie came out nearly burned and I had to rely on the granny crutch of, "Oh, grandmother is getting so forgetful in her old age." For any slip up, calling a child by the wrong name, mentioning a memory that is not the fake grandmother's but your own, it is always useful to say, "Granny's getting old, isn't she, children?" Use it too much, though, and you've got them worrying about Alzheimer's and before you know it, the parents have killed you off.

By the time the Fergusons arrive, I remember everything about them, can ask about Missy's ballet recital, Tina's pet hamster, and tell them about my trip to Ireland with a senior citizens travel company (the Fergusons wanted a globe-hopping grandmother, to help teach the kids about other places and cultures). "MeeMaw!" Tina shouts. "I got a dollar from the tooth fairy." One of her front teeth disappeared since our last visit. "Well," I say. "I can't let the tooth fairy get ahead of me," and I reach into my purse and produce two dollars for her. I will have to include this in my report, verified by the parents in their own report, if I want to be reimbursed. And I will want to be reimbursed.

After dinner, we look at photos of my trip to Ireland, mostly landscapes and buildings with a few pictures where I have been digitally inserted into the scene. The kids ask if they can come with me on my next trip and I tell them that these trips are only for old people. "Then come with us on our next vacation," says Missy, who then looks at her father. Mr. Ferguson shrugs his shoulders and then says, "I think we could arrange that." Free vacations are a rare bonus; Martha always gets free vacations.

As they leave, I hug the children. I touch each of Tina's teeth, making sure there are no other loose ones. She giggles and leans into me. Missy then hops onto the sofa and hugs me, and when no one is looking, I slip two dollars into her pocket, placing my finger to my lips so that she won't say anything about it. As they walk out the door, the parents thank me for letting them come over. "Anytime," I say, happy for the few hours of their company. While some parents will address me only through the children—"Say good-bye to your grandmother, kids, and thank her for the wonderful meal"—Mr. Ferguson calls me Mom and hugs me as if I were his real mother. As I wave to them from the porch, Missy spins away from her parents and runs back to me. "I love you, MeeMaw," she says, and I tell her that that I love her too. And the truth of this strikes me so much that it takes almost four hours before I can forget about them, placing each photo back in the box, reminding myself the entire time that I love four other families as well.

○○

At the main office, I meet with my arranger and he gives me the details of the new project. The family is newly wealthy, people who dipped into the Internet boom and left before it fell apart. They are now, it must be said, loaded, which is why they can afford weekly meetings with a stand-in. "So," I ask him, still unable to shake my curiosity, "why is this job being outsourced? What did the old lady do that was so bad?" The arranger shakes his head. "Probably best not to think about it," he says but I remind him that I am a professional and in order to be effective, I need to anticipate possible problems, avoid the same fate. "It's complicated," he says. "I am sure that it is," I reply. Finally, he explains.

The Beamer family wants to start clean. They have a young child and new wealth and they want to forget their past life, which was, although not terrible, not great either. The husband sails and climbs mountains now, the mother does yoga and charity functions. The child is learning Japanese. It is all very impressive. What is not impressive, however, is the grandmother. Without making the Beamers out to be too callous, the grandmother is simply, well, boring.

Two years ago, the grandmother slipped on some icy steps and broke her hip. The Beamers had to put her in a home. Recently, she had a stroke. The child, a little girl who is six years old, has not seen the grandmother since her removal to the retirement facility. The parents fear what the stress of seeing her grandmother in such a state would do to her. So they want to start fresh, with a grandmother that the child can interact with and form fond memories of that will last a lifetime.

"So, basically," I say, still wondering if I can do this, "the Beamers are evil."

"That's not fair. These days, it's not enough to have a grandparent," he reminds me. "They have to be fun; they have to enrich everyone else's lives in some way. Familial obligations are going the way of the buffalo."

"Good for us."

"Very good for us," he says. "This works out okay, switching out for grandparents that aren't even dead, we might just have a new market angle."

"Trade-ins," I say.

"I like that," he says, nodding.

I don't say anything for a while, flip through the file he has given me. Do I really want to sink this low? And then I think about the child. Shouldn't she be allowed a wonderful grandmother? Aren't I a wonderful grandmother, however fake I may be? And a small part of me, no matter how much I hate it, is interested in the challenge, a switch, a magic trick, taking over and improving upon something.

"You hate them, don't you?" he says.

"Yes."

"You're going to make them love you, aren't you?" he asks.

"Yes," I say. "Yes, I am."

⁛

I have dinner with Cal, who is sixty-four years old, and one of the best stand-ins. He has fourteen families, six more than the next closest stand-in. He fills a very impressive, high-demand role: decorated war hero, retired doctor, and a champion over-sixty marathon runner. It is a lethal combination. He is also, for reasons I do not question, quite fond of me. "Where were you when I was a younger man?" he sometimes asks. "You were too busy," I tell him. "You wouldn't have even noticed me."

Cal is not happy about my new fam. He has very specific ideas about the ethics of this business. He always includes personal stories from the actual grandfather's life, an attempt to provide the child with some sense of their actual family history. He spaces visits to his families far apart to allow himself time to decompress, to remember each visit—though I tease him that this is merely an excuse for his terrible disconnect skills. And he wouldn't, under any circumstances, do a switch job.

"Then why do it at all?" I ask him. "You don't need the money."

"No, I don't need the money," he says. "But I need people to want me. I need to be of use."

I don't know how to respond so I just sip my drink.

"Stay with me tonight?" he asks.

"All right," I tell him.

As we leave, I suddenly remember something and run to the pay phone in the lobby. "I just have to call one of my grandchildren," I say, "and convince him that I'm still alive."

∷

I meet Mr. and Mrs. Beamer later in the week, what the company calls "a meet and greet," though it is much more than that. We have to agree on the specifics of the contract, go over the level of involvement, smooth out any possible backstory problems, and try to establish a preliminary bond with one another, so it will seem authentic to the child. It is also the last chance, for either the stand-in or the parents, to back out before the child is notified of the "new" grandparent. Before I walk into the room, I take all of my emotions that may cause problems during this session, all of my misgivings about the project, and get rid of them. I imagine placing them on an ice floe and pushing them out into the water, waving good-bye, though I am quite sure they won't be coming back. And when that is accomplished, when I am ready, I go meet these people that I supposedly love so much.

The Beamers are very attractive, very polite, and very enthusiastic about the possibility of my becoming a part of their family. Though I fear disliking them, I see enough good points to know how to work around it. "We know this is strange," Mr. Beamer says. "We thought about this a couple of years ago," and I nearly flinch because I remember that this is when the grandmother broke her hip, but I keep smiling. "But we had to weigh the options and decide if we wanted Greta to have access to something like this." They are both grinning at me so I say, "Well, I think the pros outweigh the cons by an overwhelming percentage. I think you'll find this to be even more true after a few outings, when you get to see how well Greta responds to this new presence in her life." They both nod, encouraged, reassured of their own decision-making skills, their know-how, their ability to take a problematic situation and fix it.

"Well," Mr. Beamer says, looking hopefully at his wife, who is nodding, "I think we can wholeheartedly say that we are very happy to have you become a part of our family," and I lean forward to shake his hand. Then he finishes the sentence, "Mom." Both of them laugh, and my eyes go to slits, but I am still smiling, still moving my hand toward him. He shakes it and I am counting the seconds until I can leave. I feel all the anger and guilt about this job returning, emotions that will become problematic if not repressed.

°°
°°

"How is this different?" asks Martha, nearly drunk on gin and tonics, a book held upside-down in her hands. "I still don't understand the problem."

"She's not dead," Angela, another stand-in, says, exasperated.

"She is to us."

"But not to them," Angela responds.

"No," I say. "She's dead to them too. That's the problem."

"It shouldn't be," says Martha.

"It won't be," I say, though I still can't shake the doubt, feel I am getting out of practice.

°°
°°

A week later, backstory rehearsed and rerehearsed, I sign out one of the cars from the main office, a gray Cadillac—all the stand-ins' cars are Cadillacs or Oldsmobiles—and drive the twenty-five minutes to the Beamers' house. For the first visit, it seemed easier for the child, Greta, to meet on familiar ground. I pull into the driveway, stare into the rearview mirror until I am happy with the expression on my face, and walk to the door, where the Beamers are waiting: husband, wife, daughter. "Grandma's here!" shouts Mrs. Beamer and I nod, still smiling, and say, "I certainly am." The Beamers nudge the girl toward me. "Say hello to your grandmother," Mr. Beamer says. Greta is having none of this.

She holds onto her father, hiding behind one of his legs. "Say hello," her father repeats, but she moves entirely behind him. "You remember Grandma?" I say, deciding that she needs to hear my voice and see that I am not dangerous before she commits. She peeks out at me and I get to see her. She is prettier than her picture had prepared me for, blond curls, big blue eyes, like a fake child that someone would make in order to convince people to have children. "You look different," she says, and I see Mr. Beamer about to say something, something that will not help the situation, and I respond, "You look different too. You were just a little thing the last time I saw you. You look so grown up, I can hardly believe I'm looking at the same girl."

She steps out from behind her father and walks up to me. I'm not going to force her into a hug, but I know it would look good, would reassure the parents. "You don't remember Grandma?" I say, and she stares at me so hard that I have to remind myself not to pull back. And then she leans forward, puts her little arms around my neck, and I know it will only get easier now, that things will fall into a familiar rhythm. We are a family.

○○
○○

One of Martha's families killed her off. She is stunned, shaken beyond what I would have expected. We all anticipate being killed off at one point or another. Once the child becomes older, and visits to the grandparents are a chore more than a treat, parents tend to move into the next critical stage of family experience: death. It is a strange experience, to be informed by your arranger that a family has decided to downsize. The child, now older, experiences the finality of death but maintains the memories of you, which is what the parents wanted in the first place. They take out notices in the obituaries, have funerals, place an urn on the mantle. And we just wait for another family to take their place. But Martha was taken in her prime, suddenly removed from a fam, and this distresses her to the point that she is drinking so much that a few of her other fams are worried.

"I didn't deserve to be killed," she says. "Nothing I possibly did was enough to deserve death."

"Death is natural," I tell her. "We all die."

"Maybe you do," she spits. "I was so good, fams were going to keep me until I outlived all of them. They were going to be leaving me money in their wills."

"At least it was sudden," Eugenia says. "You didn't have to provide foreshadowing. No dizzy spells, a tumble in the shower, something mysterious on an X-ray."

"How did you go?" I ask.

"Oh, this was the worst," Martha says. "In my sleep. Peaceful."

"That's nice, though," Angela says.

"I wanted a skydiving accident," Martha says. "I wanted a bank robbery gone bad."

"It's just part of the job," I say. "These are the things we have to deal with."

"Well," says Martha, taking another sip from her drink. "We're getting too old for this. We're too old to have to deal with dying."

⠛

I spend another evening at the Beamers' house. Greta and I play a board game where you move your piece around a giant mall and buy things with a gold credit card. Everything seems way too expensive and I can't justify the cost, so I lose, which is good. Grandma should always lose. The Beamers have been gone since I arrived, hidden away somewhere in the house. Even when they come to my house, they step out to make a phone call or remember an errand they need to run. I am beginning to think that they might just want a babysitter, and not a grandmother, but I'm not going to be the one to tell them that.

Greta, on the other hand, is wonderful. I listen to her count out numbers in Japanese—*itchykneesunshego*—so fast that she cannot possibly understand what she is saying, which is pleasing to me. I like the fact that she may be forced into older pursuits, but she is not succeeding quite so easily, that she is still a child. I make a cat's cradle with yarn and it takes her a very long time before she puts her hand through it, her eyes wide open. When I complete the trick, she laughs so suddenly, so loud, that I laugh just as loudly. It is a good laugh, and I remind myself to practice that laugh for other fams.

I watch a video with Greta, which I find incredibly disconcerting but she sings right along with the giant blobs of color that dance around the screen. When she grows tired, she climbs into my lap and rests her head against my chest. I rock her slowly until I realize I need to get home, that I have to prepare for the Mead fam, who will be arriving this weekend. But I sit a few more minutes, reluctant to wake her, until I can't put it off any longer.

"Can you sing me the lullaby?" Greta asks me as I am tucking her into bed. I freeze.

"What lullaby?" I ask sweetly, while in my head I am furiously sifting through the information for this song. Am I becoming forgetful? Am I losing my touch?

"I don't know what it is," she says, "but you sang it to me before."

An image flashes in my head of Greta and her real grandmother, a lullaby, two people who really care about each other. I shake it off.

"Well, Greta, your grandma is becoming forgetful in her old age. I'll have to think about it. How about this one though?"

I sing "Goodnight, Irene," and my voice sounds too low, not delicate enough, and I make a mental note to sign up for singing classes at the community center. When Greta finally falls asleep, I kiss her softly on the cheek and walk out of the room. "Sweet dreams," I say, but of course she can't hear me. I just want to say it.

I walk down the stairs, into the exercise room, where the Beamers are riding machines to infinity.

"You never mentioned the song," I tell them.

"What?" they say in unison, the sound of their machines slowing down.

"The song," I say, a little overexcited, "the fuc—the lullaby that I used to sing to her."

"I don't recall there ever being a lullaby," says Mrs. Beamer. "Greta might be imagining things."

"If you aren't providing me with all the information," I tell them, trying to remain calm, "this could fall apart and everyone would be very unhappy. If Greta had a more detailed level of previous interaction that I wasn't told about—"

"Mom," says Mr. Beamer, "I assure you that we are invested in this as much as you, even more so."

"So you'll get me that song?" I ask.

"Oh, well, I don't know how we could do that," he says, almost stammering.

"Well, I think I know how we could do that," I say and then I remember who I am, an employee, and who they are, my client, and I brush the hair out of my face and smile. "I'm sorry," I say. "Greta has been happy with me, I trust?"

"Oh, she loves you," says Mrs. Beamer, her machine back in full swing.

"I'll make sure it stays that way. And I won't bother you with these small details anymore."

"Thanks, Mom," Mr. Beamer says, and I walk back to my car and disconnect from the love I feel for the Beamers, which is incredibly easy. Then I disconnect from Greta, and, though it takes the entire car ride back to the main office, I have forgotten her as well. By the time I make it home, all I am thinking about is that lullaby. I tell myself that it is purely to improve job performance, that I need this song to fully establish my position as "grandmother," but there is a small part of me that wants something else. I want to meet the grandmother.

⁙

We are required to have monthly physicals to ensure that we are healthy enough to be grandparents. The company needs lead time if something unexpected turns up.

"You having any problems lately, any new sources of stress?" my doctor asks, tapping his pencil on my chart. "I have constant sources of stress," I say. "Tina's hamster died. We talked for an hour last night, unscheduled." He taps the chart one more time. "High blood pressure," he says. "High blood pressure can go all kinds of ways. Watch it. Calm down." I am calm. I am so calm that I don't even feel nervous when I leave the doctor's office, take the walkway to my family arranger, sit down in front of him, and ask him for the Beamer grandmother's address.

"Crazy," he says. "That is crazy and you are not crazy. You're a pro."

"I just want to observe," I tell him. "I need to find some gestures, turns of phrases, that will help keep the child invested and unsuspicious."

"The kid is suspicious?" he asks, almost jumping out of his seat.

"No," I shout. "She's fine. She loves me. They all love me. I just need to see the grandmother. I need to get a lullaby—"

"What?"

"A lullaby that the girl remembers her grandmother singing. The parents are drawing a complete blank. Just let me have the address."

"What makes you think I have it?" he asks.

"You have it."

He nods and turns his computer screen toward me, types a few commands, and there it is.

"I could lose my job if this gets out," he tells me.

"I'm a pro," I say. "I could make this lady think that I'm *her* grandmother."

He doesn't laugh. "Don't do that," he says. "Just get the lullaby and leave."

∞

"Who do you love better," Peter, one of the McAllister children, asks, "me or Julie?" Julie climbs onto the sofa, too, eager for my answer. "I love both of you in equal amounts," I tell them.

"I love all of my grandchildren exactly the same." Which is the truest thing I've ever said.

○○
○○

Cal is in my bed tonight. "We should do some couples work sometime," he says. "A lot of families want both grandparents now. There's one fam right now that has all four grandparents contracted through the company." I kiss him, shut him up, and then I say, "Come with me to visit this woman." He shakes his head. "No," he says. "I don't want to be a party to that." I tell him that I need to see her. If I can see her and not get discouraged, not feel like the worst person in the world, I keep telling myself that I'll be even better at my job, that nothing will keep me from being anything less than a perfect grandmother.

"We should just quit," he tells me. "Get away from all this and be normal."

"The money is good," I tell him.

"I have money," he says.

"I like the work," I say. "It's challenging."

"You don't like the work," he says.

"Well, I like the moments when I forget that it's work."

"That's what other people experience all the time."

"No it isn't," I say. "That's why people pay us money to love them."

○○
○○

"I'm a friend of the family," I tell the nurse at the retirement home. "An old family friend."

She nods and leads me down the hallway. The ease of this astounds me at first but then I realize that people will believe anything, are looking for an excuse to believe what you say.

Mrs. Beamer is sitting up in her bed when I see her, and I almost turn around and walk out of the building. She looks nothing like me, thin, wispy white hair and deep, sunken eyes, and somehow this makes me feel strange. I wonder how Greta could possibly mistake the two of us, but almost immediately I feel a sense of pride at making such a convincing switch. She smiles when I walk in, and I smile back. When the nurse leaves, Mrs. Beamer's smile fades a little, becomes confused, and she asks me, "I'm sorry, but who are you?" I start to answer but I have no idea what to say. "A friend of the family," I say, finally, and she smiles again. "That's nice," she says.

I tell her that her family asked me to come visit, to let her know how they are doing. "They miss you," I say. "Well, I miss them too," she says. "I don't see them as much as I'd like." I pull out a few photos of Greta that I have taken, pictures I think a grandmother would want to see. "Who is this?" she asks, and I feel so sad that she must be regressing even more quickly in this place. "It's Greta," I tell her. "Your granddaughter?" She shakes her head. "That's not my Greta," she says and I don't have the heart to argue with her. She reaches toward her nightstand and hands me a picture frame. "That's Greta," she says, and points to a small girl with blond hair and her two front teeth missing, standing between Mr. and Mrs. Beamer. It is not Greta.

I feel dizzy, cannot quite understand how to proceed. "This is your granddaughter?" I ask, and she nods. "She visits you?" I ask, and again she nods. "Once a month," she says. "My son and his wife are very busy with their careers so they have a driver bring Greta to see me and we have a wonderful time together, just the two of us here in the room. Isn't she beautiful?" I respond that she is, trying to piece this together, and then I understand. The idea is perfect, and I immediately feel sick. Child stand-ins. A double-switch.

"Are you all right?" Mrs. Beamer asks me, but I don't respond. I can only think of a little girl sitting in a car on her way to this nursing home. I imagine her taking what little she knows about family and love and leaving them in the car while she goes inside to see her grandmother whom she has never met before. I always think that what I do is so hard, but maybe it isn't. Maybe it's the easiest thing in the world.

"Excuse me," Mrs. Beamer says, still trying to get my attention.

"Yes?" I say finally, remembering there is someone else in the room, wanting nothing more than to leave.

"Did you need anything? Why did you come see me?"

I remember why I am here and try to recover. "Well," I tell her, "I wanted to see if I could hear you sing the lullaby, for Greta."

"Oh, I suppose so. She hasn't asked me to do that in a long time."

I take out my tape recorder and she sings, softly, something about the moon being made of old green cheese. It isn't particularly good, but she sings it as if it means something, and I know that it does. When she is finished, I turn off the recorder and leave.

"Tell them to come soon," she says, but I don't say anything.

⁸⁸

One stand-in quit after only a few months. "I feel like a prostitute," she said.

"Oh please," Martha answered, "Prostitutes have it easy."

⠔

I knock on the Beamers' door until Mr. Beamer shows.

"Oh, hi, Mom." He frowns, touches his finger to his temple. "Do we have something scheduled for today?"

"I saw someone today."

"Who?"

"Your mother."

"Well, you shouldn't have done that."

"Why?" I ask him. "Why would you set your daughter up with a new grandmother and give your mother a new grandchild?"

"We should talk about this another time," he says, clearly annoyed. "Or perhaps we shouldn't talk about this at all."

"It's ridiculous."

"No," he says, getting angry. "It's not ridiculous at all. We wanted Greta to have a grandmother who could enrich her life, who could do the things that my mother simply can't do. So we gave Greta the best grandmother we could find."

"Me," I say.

"You," he answers. "But I love my mother so we found a child stand-in who visits once a month and, from what we read in the stand-in's monthly reports and from the letters my mother sends us, she makes my mother very happy. Everything works out. Greta can be shy, reticent to engage with people. This girl, she's been on TV; she's amazing. Just like you. We wanted the best for our family and we got it."

"You never visit her?" I ask.

"It would only complicate things," he says. "Just because someone is related to you doesn't mean they're best suited to loving you. There's no good reason for me to keep seeing her."

"But she's your mother," I tell him.

He frowns and says, "No she isn't. You are." He shakes his head, as if I am a child and he is growing tired of explaining.

"Not for long," I say.

He glances at his watch. "Look," he says. "You are the best, but you aren't the only grandmother around. We can get another one."

"It wouldn't work twice."

"It's easy enough," he says. "We're getting pretty good at it."

We are both silent, daring the other to flinch. I imagine the call to my family arranger from the Beamers, what a poor report will do to my future contracts. Mostly, though, I hate to admit to someone like Mr. Beamer that it is hard to be fired, to be told you are no longer necessary, that there is nothing you can give to make people want you. No matter what I think of them, I want the Beamers to love me.

"Okay," I finally say. "Sorry. I'm just out of sorts."

"Hey, that's what families do," he says, and then he hugs me. "We're there for each other."

I ask if I can see Greta and he lets me in. I go upstairs and Greta is already in bed, but she sits up and smiles when she sees me come in. "Grandma!" she says, and I sit beside her. I tell her that I made a tape for her and I hand her the recorder. I hit play and we listen to her grandmother sing the lullaby. "That's it," she says, clapping her hands. She listens for a few seconds and then says, "This is you?" I nod. "And you can play it anytime you want," I say, "and think of me." We play the song again and then she is asleep.

I walk downstairs and open the front door. "Bye, Mom," both of the Beamers call out, and I am gone.

I tell Cal about the situation.

"That's horrible," he says.

"Yes," I answer, "I am."

"I'm coming over," he says, but I won't let him. I need to be alone, to think.

"I love you," he tells me.

"Oh, please don't say that word," I respond, and I hang up.

∞

After I talk to Cal, I take out the boxes for each fam and line them up in the hallway. Looking at all of them, all the pieces of other people's lives that are partly mine, I think of how empty the house would be without them. Once I began restructuring my life for the job, I got rid of items in my house that were unique to me, were too far afield from my grandmother persona. I never thought to hang on to them, and so, when all of my families kill me off, my house will be emptier than it was before I started working.

The first time I was killed off, which was very early in my career, I kept the fam's boxes for weeks after they dissolved our contract. I told the family arranger, when he asked for the information to be returned, that I wanted to keep it so I could continue to keep track of all the different families, so I wouldn't mistake one for another. "They're not going to bring you back from the dead," he warned me, which immediately made me angry. "I know that," I said. "And I'm not waiting for them to bring me back. I just want to make sure I don't mess up the families I have left." And so he let me keep the boxes.

A few weeks later, small details that I had memorized for the job were still popping into my head, little, useless things that made the family unique, like what the little girl liked for breakfast, how the boy inverted words when he was excited. When it kept happening, I said to myself, "They're not your family anymore," and I froze, my heart shifting slightly inside of me. "They were never your family," I then said. The next day I returned the boxes.

⁙

It is two in the morning, but I page my family arranger anyway. In a few minutes, he calls me back.

"This better be good," he says, stifling a yawn.

"Kill me," I say.

"I'm sure I must be dreaming. I'm sure I didn't hear that."

"Kill me off," I say.

"Look," he says, his voice now losing the edge of sleep. "Let's discuss this in the morning. You don't like the Beamers. Fine. I don't like the Beamers either, but I'll see what I can do to find someone who does. You are dead to the Beamers. Happy?"

"Kill me off entirely," I say. "I don't want to be a grandmother anymore."

"Listen, you have no idea what kind of a problem that would create, not just for you and me, but for the whole company. I can't let you do that."

"I can call the families myself," I tell him. "I could tell a thing or two to my grandchildren."

"Well, that's just mean," he says. "That's completely unethical."

"Kill me off."

There is silence on his end of the line, a minute passes.

"You can't come back," he says.

"Fine."

"Okay," he says, weary. "You're dead. I'll send out the notices tomorrow. Rest in peace."

⁚⁚

I sit in my study, alone. I don't feel dead. I think about what will happen tomorrow, the parents shouting at my family arranger, exasperated with the love they have paid good money for and must now forfeit. They will gather their children, tell them about Grandma or Mimi or Gammy. The children will cry, will need to be reassured that this is how life is. We are born, we live, and then we die.

Finally alone in my house that is only mine, I allow myself to understand that I am not leaving these families but losing them. And it is strangely wonderful to feel the lack of something instead of believing that it was never there in the first place. I walk into the hallway and begin moving each fam's box back into the study. Years from now, when the children are older, I wonder if they will remember me at all, if they will even be able to picture my face. I wonder if they will remember how much I loved each and every single one of them, because they were my own, as if we were all one big, happy, perfect family.

blowing up on the spot

i count my steps because I have a boring and unhappy life. Each day, I walk to my job at the factory, placing one foot in front of the other and assigning a number for each step. It calms me and helps make my life more tolerable. I have walked from the apartment I share with my brother all the way to the factory in only seven thousand and forty-five steps. Each day I try out new paths, taking longer strides, choosing my steps carefully. It is a game, albeit a pathetic and queer game, that provides me with some kind of happiness. Thinking in sequence gives time meaning. It keeps me from exploding. It fills my head for a while, keeps me from thinking unhappy thoughts, before I wait in a queue outside the factory and file into the sorting room, where it rains letters of the alphabet for eight hours.

I am a sorter at the Scrabble factory, the primary producer of

Scrabble tiles for Hasbro Inc. There are five large sorting rooms in the factory, each one filled with one hundred workers who sort through a mountain of wooden tiles, which fall in clumps from an overhead chute. At several times during the day, a large blue light flickers on and off, accompanied by a siren's wail, and all the workers stop their sorting, pick themselves up off their hands and knees, and watch *A*'s and *J*'s and *R*'s fall all around them, making *tic-tic* sounds like a thousand typewriters going at once. I wade around in the alphabet, up to my knees, and search for *Q*'s. It is not a glamorous job.

In every game of Scrabble, there is one *Q*, a single opportunity for a *quack* or a *quarter* or a *quibble*. In a ratio, for every one hundred letters, there is one *Q*. So sorting through a thousand tiles will leave me with only ten *Q*'s, and since we are paid just a tiny hourly wage and are given a bonus for each assigned letter we collect each day, it is understandable why I do not like my job. I have been collecting *Q*'s for almost three years, since I was twenty years old, and even though I have become quite good at it, I run my hands over the wooden tiles and touch the *E*'s and *N*'s and *A*'s with the tips of my fingers and dream of holding them.

⁚⁚

Today, I manage to find fifty-three *Q*'s. Yesterday I found forty; two days before that I found sixty-three. Like most good sorters, I'm able to Braille my *Q*'s, dipping my hands into a sea of letters and moving my fingertips over the tiles until I can feel a *Q*. It's a lot easier than turning over each tile and then tossing it aside. Everyone is moving quickly, running to one area and pulling up handfuls of tiles before moving to a new space. The woman who collects blanks, a new worker who started two days ago, is so frustrated she is throwing handfuls of tiles in the air. Close beside her, a young man with bloodshot eyes and a two days' growth of beard is looking for defective tiles without any letters on them. They fight constantly for tiles, walking home from work with bruises and very little money in their pockets.

At the end of work today, the quitting bell rings and we line up. I notice the *M* woman still on her hands and knees, her face streaked red from crying. When I walk over to her, she holds up a handful of tiles, all *W*'s. "They look the same, Leonard," she tells me, almost pleading. "I mean, if you didn't look too closely." She's spent the entire day picking up the wrong letter, and once the *W* man understands what has happened, he runs over with a huge smile on his face. Just before he reaches her, she tosses her tiles across the room, mixing them in with the unsorted piles, and the *W* man dives toward them, screaming. As I walk out of the factory, I punch my time card, drop off my collected tiles for the day, and begin counting the steps home.

Seven thousand, three hundred and eighty-three.

⁘

I live in a small apartment above a confection stop. The shop is run by Hedy, an older woman with salt-and-pepper hair pinned up in a tight bun and kind features that seem as if she has never known anger. She lives with her daughter in a small apartment in the back of the shop and charges my brother and me one hundred dollars a month for the apartment above them. We have been here for three months now, slowly getting used to the new surroundings, of waking every morning to the smell of cinnamon and sugar rising from the floor like steam. I walk into the shop and purchase a handful of lemon drops for a dollar and a mint-flavored lollipop for a quarter for my brother. As I pay, Hedy's nineteen-year-old daughter, Joan, emerges from the kitchen carrying a tray of chocolate turtles.

Joan's hair is shiny black and falls past her shoulders. Her eyes gleam brown like caramel and when she catches my gaze, her smile creeps across her face in small increments, as if her happiness starts in one place and slowly moves out in all directions. She holds up one of the chocolate turtles and lets me take a bite. Pecans, chocolate, and caramel mix together in my mouth and I taste Joan's fingerprints on my tongue. She is beautiful, brushing hair out of her eyes, and I want to stand there for hours and watch her, but the shop is beginning to fill with rush-hour customers. They come in every day for a sugar fix after a long shift at one of the factories in the neighborhood. I walk up the steps to the apartment, fifteen steps, and press my ear against the door, listening for movement, for my brother's presence. I can hear him in there, swimming in the living room.

Caleb is in the middle of the living room, lying facedown on a long, narrow piece of wood suspended by two chairs, practicing his strokes with weighted bands on his wrists. He is swinging his arms over his head, his fingers pulled tightly together to cut down on wind resistance. His body is pale, almost translucent from lack of sun, and his muscles spasm violently under his skin with each movement. When he notices me, he stops his swimming motion and smiles. I am tired, my fingertips are sore, and I fall easily onto the couch, ready for sleep. Caleb rolls off the board and crawls on hands and knees over to me, resting his forehead against mine.

Caleb is sixteen. He goes to the public school eight blocks away and is the star swimmer on the team. After his classes, he practices at the YMCA with the rest of the team until four, and when I return from work an hour and a half later, the apartment is already filled with the smell of chlorine, of chemicals. He has shaved his head and his eyebrows to swim faster at his next meet. When he stares at me with his pale blue eyes, stained red from the chlorine, he looks like a seal, like a newborn puppy.

"Guess how many steps it took to get home today," I say. We play this game every day.

"I don't know . . . a billion," he replies.

"Less."

"Two."

"More."

"A million."

"Less."

"A thousand."

"More."

"A hundred thousand."

"Less."

"Five thousand."

"More."

"Ten thousand."

"Less."

"Seven thousand."

"More."

"Eight thousand."

"Less."

"Seven thousand three hundred and eighty- . . . four."

"Almost . . . seven thousand three hundred and eighty-three."

"Did you count the step into the shop from outside?"

"No."

"Well. There you go."

Caleb lies facedown on the carpet beside the couch. He

keeps his head turned away from me and his arms at his sides with the palms up. I rest on my back with one arm hanging off the couch, tracing circles on his skin, dry and scaly from too much exposure to the chemically treated water. With his arms positioned the way they are, I can see the scars on his wrists, the deep wounds covered with new skin. Caleb has tried to kill himself twice in the three years since our parents died. The last time, he slit his wrists with a Swiss Army knife during practice and dove in the pool to swim a hundred-meter freestyle, trailing a cloud of blood behind him. He spent three weeks in the hospital and the doctors say that he seems fine now, but they said that the last time. He is not an unhappy person, just unstable, and that's more unsettling. At work, while searching for Q's, I will feel something move quick and light up my spine and think of Caleb. I spend as much time as possible watching him, keeping an eye on him, but the fact is that if he wants to do it again, he will. It's an impossible urge to quell.

∷

Three years ago, my parents blew up. I don't know how else to say it. One evening, riding the subway home from an evening out, my parents sat in an empty subway car and spontaneously combusted. A subway guard found them later that night, the upper half of their bodies charred beyond recognition. It was the first recorded double spontaneous human combustion in history, which we unfortunately heard several times over the following weeks. Their death was featured in a special hour-long episode *of Luminous Mysteries of the Unexplained*, but I didn't watch. It's horrible when you lose both of your parents, even worse when you can't explain it. When people ask now, I usually say they died in a fire or a gas explosion. They are gone, and I can accept that, or at least I'm trying to. What I can't get around is the question of whether it could happen to me.

I wonder if spontaneous combustion is hereditary, if it can be passed down from generation to generation and lies waiting to make itself known. Perhaps it's like Huntington's disease, a fifty-fifty chance and you have to wait until you get older to find out. At work, I'll be sorting tiles and feel flush, red-cheeked, and my heart will stop, waiting to explode. Most nights I sit in bed for hours, lying perfectly still and waiting for a sound, like a pop, like an electrical spark or a fizz. Or I sit out on the fire escape and have waking dreams of shooting up into the air and exploding like a firework, spreading myself across the sky in multiple colors.

I am sitting on the fire escape tonight, drinking a glass of milk and eating a chocolate drop. The sky is clogged with too much smoke, and I watch the moonlight make shadows through the clouds. I look at the alley behind the shop and try to figure out how many steps it would take to walk through it, end to end. I am pacing the steps in my head when I hear Joan below me, climbing up the ladder. This has been happening for two weeks now, these night meetings. She is even more beautiful at night, when her hair is lost in the night's darkness, mixes with it, and her face seems to be hovering in front of me. We sit on the fire escape, legs hanging over the edge, and she rests her head on my shoulder. She smells of sweat and burned sugar, of a fancy dessert that you set on fire, cherries flambé. I tell her about work, about how many steps it took to get home. While she listens, she plucks a strand of hair from her head and chews on it, as if it were a blade of grass.

She does this often, a habit of sorts, and this time I ask her about it, twirl her hair around one of my fingers. She smiles, takes another piece of her hair, and offers it to me. I take it, hold it up to the moonlight, and then place it gently on my tongue. It is sweet, like a piece of string coated with rock candy. She tells me it is from working in the candy shop all day. Clouds of sugar hover in the air and settle in her hair. I chew the flavor from the strand and place the hair in my pocket.

I ask her if she is happy spending so much time at the shop. She has been working there with her mother since she was a child, skipping school altogether and not doing any of the normal things young women do. But she tells me that she likes it, that when her mother goes, she will take over the shop. "It's one thing I know how to do," she tells me. "It's imprinted I guess." I notice the time and realize that I must get to bed, even if I just lie awake until I go to work. Joan kisses me, quick, her tongue flicking across my front teeth, and she turns to climb back down. I watch her move down the ladder, down the twenty-four rungs, and creep back into her room. My face is hot, warm. Even after she is gone, I wait out on the fire escape for it to pass, trying not to explode.

⁞⁞

To unlock the potential power of the letter *Q*, one must learn quickly that there are other words to spell than those that have the standard *qu* structure like *quartet* and *quality* and *queen*. *Qat, qaid, qoph,* and *faqir* will all do the trick. While I work, it takes everything I have to make *Q* important, to think of it as something more than the seventeenth letter of the alphabet. And I have to do it. I have to think that there is some reason that I am searching so hard for this letter to the point that my fingers ache at night with phantom pains, the outline of a *Q* pressing into my fingertips.

∷

I steal a letter today at work. *Q* after *Q* after *Q* and my fingertips finally find something else. I Braille a new letter, holding a *J* between my thumb and forefinger. Its line is smooth, an elegant curve at the bottom that my fingertip traces like a car going around a bend. I want it. I want to give it to Joan, to follow it up with an *O* and an *A* and an *N* until I can lay her name out in front of her. I look around, see the *J* woman, her hair hanging loose over her eyes, and I quickly shove the tile into my pocket. A lot of workers steal letters. Some people, over a period of time, take enough letters so that they can play the game at home, on a piece of cardboard lined with a ruler. At the end of work, I reach into my pocket and find the *J* again. As I move to the counter to turn in my tiles, I slip the *J* under my tongue, hold it there even after I walk out onto the sidewalk. I keep it there as I count the number of steps, thinking of Joan and hiding her in my mouth.

∷

At night, when I am trying not to explode, when I am trying not to spend the entire night listening for the sound of my brother breathing, so many images of my parents in that subway car pop into my head. It's different every time.

Here's one way that I see it: They are coming home from a night out, a meal at some diner, a movie, a milkshake afterward, and then they are side by side in an empty subway car. My father says something rude, something he knows he shouldn't mention, but decides to do so anyway. My mother mutters something back to him, *bastard, son of a bitch,* something like that. My father shifts slightly in his seat, turning away from her, trying very hard not to say something he is very sure that he will regret later. They are both angry, both thinking up caustic, mean things to say to each other. My father's face is dark red, almost purple, like it gets when he takes apart some appliance in our house and then realizes he has no idea how to put it back together. His head aches, his stomach burns a little, but he chalks it up to greasy diner food. My mother feels flush, attributes it to adrenaline, from thinking of different ways to maim my father. The subway grows increasingly warm, it gets harder to breathe. My parents look at each other for just a second, realize they do not love each other, do not want to get off at the same stop together, and they explode. That's one way I see it.

⁛

I get back home from work, seven thousand nine hundred and fifty-four steps, and Caleb and Joan are sitting out in front of the shop. Caleb is talking excitedly, moving his hands around in front of his face and rocking back and forth. Joan listens, frowning, and when they see me, both of them spring up. Caleb grabs my arm, pulls me inside the shop and up the stairs while Joan follows behind. We sit on the couch, all three squeezed together, while we pass around a bag of multicolored gumdrops. "It's the news, Leonard," he says to me. "Watch this," and Caleb turns up the volume of the TV.

A woman in Canton, Ohio, spontaneously combusted last night. Her neighbors found her this morning, a pile of ashes and undamaged extremities on her easy chair. The ceiling above her had fire damage, but a newspaper at the foot of the chair wasn't even singed. The chair was only superficially burned. A paranormal expert talks to a reporter, demonstrating how a spontaneous combustion victim explodes internally, leaving the surroundings virtually unharmed. He burns a candle made of hog's fat to show how the body, after the initial explosion, burns it's own fat until only ashes remain, ashes that are more fine, more powdery, than cremated remains. Caleb is now off the couch, his face inches from the tiny screen. "Just like Mom and Pop," he says to no one. Joan asks me what Caleb means but I cannot tell her the specifics, not yet. I stand up and walk away, counting. I listen to the sound of Joan's footsteps behind me as she follows and I count those too.

That night, Joan lies in bed with me as I tell her about exploding. I run my hands over her chest and stomach, comforted by the sameness and differences of our bodies. She is soft, warm against my fingertips, while my own body is tight, muscular, coiled tension. Joan traces the freckles that cover my body and as her finger touches my skin, she says she can feel me vibrating. She wraps her arms tight around my waist, pulls me close to her, and I start talking.

I tell her that the most likely victim of spontaneous human combustion is a solitary woman, that 75 percent of all known cases of SHC are women. I tell her that some people believe that arsonist poltergeists are to blame, that the spirits of firestarters roam the cities setting souls on fire. In Lucknow, a little town in India, the government requested disaster relief funds for an outbreak of "spirit fires." I tell her that by manipulating internal organs, people can generate explosive bursts of electrical energy from within their stomachs. This was documented in the Blair "ring of fire" expedition to Indonesia in the early sixteenth century. I tell her that maybe people explode because they move their organs around without knowing it, that you are sitting down one day and your organs shift by accident and you blow up. I tell her all these things, but I do not tell her that I am afraid of exploding because her lips are soft against mine and I do not want her to leave me.

⁚⁚

Here is another way that I see it: My parents are riding the subway home after a beautiful night. The moon makes my mother's face shine, my father looks ten years younger. They find an empty subway car and kiss, pull each other close. They whisper things into each other's ears, run their hands over their bodies until the windows in the subway are fogged with steam. They are happy; they are in love and in the moment of this demonstration of their love, the space between them, the friction from their bodies, ignites and they explode wrapped up in each other's arms. They look into each other's eyes and a flash blinds them and the smoke from their ashes mingle together and rise up out of the subway car. That's another way I see it.

⁚⁚

I take an O at work today . . . actually, I take three of them. I am always finding them, they feel so much like a Q, and so I decide that it wouldn't really matter if I took three of them. I think about making a bracelet for Joan out of the tiles, a string around her wrist so the fine wood grain of the tiles will slide up and down her arm when she touches my face. The blue light flashes, the siren wails, and when the tiles fall, I hold out my hands and feel them fall through my fingers.

I find only twenty-nine Q's, and I wonder if someone is hiding them from me. Occasionally, if you rub someone the wrong way, they start hoarding your letters and hiding them in the corners of the room. One day, the S man, a thin, long-legged man who constantly chews on multiple sticks of licorice gum so that it looks like he has no teeth, pushed over the man who collects *R*'s. For an entire week after that, the *S* man was running around the room, searching for *S*'s and shaking his nearly empty bag of tiles. Before work ends, I check the corners of the room and decide that I just had a slow day, that the *Q*'s just didn't fall my way. When the quitting bell rings, I shove the three *O*'s into my mouth. As we walk to the counter, I catch a glimpse of myself in the reflection of a window, my mouth crooked and poking out at odd angles. I feel my face flush, a stirring in my stomach, and my feet will not move. I spit two of the *O*'s into my bag, decide to say that I must have picked them up by accident, and keep the other tile tight under my tongue. I say nothing to the worker at the counter, manage only a half smile, and begin counting my way home.

⁘

When I get back to the apartment, seven thousand three hundred and twelve steps, Joan is waiting outside on the curb. The shop is closed, the lights dim, and when I see Joan's face, I know I will not like what I hear. There was an incident at the swim meet today. Caleb is at the hospital, where Hedy is waiting until I get there. I stumble, lean up against Joan, and she helps me walk over to the hospital. I hold onto her arm, both of my hands squeezing tight. My feet shuffle slowly and it is hard to count the steps, to know where one ends and the other begins.

In the hospital room, Caleb sits upright, his lungs pushing softly against his chest. He is pale, more pale than usual, a cloudy, splotchy sheet of chalk rather than the soothing translucence he usually gives off. Hedy has gone back to the store, but Joan sits outside in the waiting room, chewing strands of her hair and asking nurses about Caleb when they walk by. I do not know if it was because of the report on the news last night, but Caleb has tried again.

Today at swim practice, when he lined up for laps, he toed the pool's edge with weight bands around his ankles and wrists. He dove into the pool with his teammates and while they thrashed and kicked waves of water into the air, Caleb, in the fourth lane, quietly sank to the bottom, pulled his knees in close to his body, and sat on the floor of the pool. It took some time—with the commotion and splashing—for Caleb's coach to notice his body underwater. It was not long, a few minutes at the most. Doctors say he is fine, has hopefully not incurred any irreversible damage. I can smell the chlorine on his body, sterile and strong like bodies after they have been embalmed, slightly plastic.

I run my fingers over the smooth streaks where his eyebrows should be and he closes his eyes. The doctors say he will not be allowed to come home for a while, that there will be tests and evaluations. His behavior is unstable and they will attempt to make it less so. I try to talk to him, but his face fills with a crooked smile, turned up too much at the corners. I think that perhaps this is what he wants, these small moments after he's tried, when the world around him is fuzzy and warm and slow.

I do not know what to say to him, and so I hold his hand to my face, breathe in his smell. He tells me before I leave that he's sorry for making me worry, that he is fine, and will be fine. "I guess I just keep doing stupid things," he says softly to me. "It's just something I do." Even though I know this, cannot quite accept it, I know that I will wait for him to come home, will smile when he does. And we will wait all over again because that's the way it works.

tunneling to the center of the earth

⚬⚬

I wake up in my own room later that night. I do not remember the walk back from the hospital, how many steps it took, if I took steps at all or just appeared in my room. Joan lies beside me, pressing her hand against my forehead. My head is on fire, fevered, and Joan's hand feels cool against my face. I sit up, lean back against the headboard of the bed, and she takes her hand away. It is dark outside; not even the faint glow of moonlight reaches the window of my room. There is nothing here except the two of us, and the things inside of me. It is too hard to hold back and so I tell Joan about my parents, about exploding.

I tell her that I am going to blow up one day, that I will be walking down the street, caught in mid-count, and I will burn a circle into the sidewalk. My head hurts. I am dizzy. I do not want to think about numbers of steps or letters or smells of sugar and chlorine or anything. I am going to explode. Pieces of me will burst like a balloon. Shreds of me will flutter to the ground, but what is inside, the air, will rush out and dissipate into the atmosphere. Joan only pulls me closer. I hide my face in her hair, hold on to her, and wait for another day to start.

⚬⚬

When the morning comes, Joan is still here with me. The idea of this, the nearness of her, makes me forget for a little while that I am not at work, which is where I am supposed to be. I have never missed a day of work. It is not something that I had ever considered the possibility of. I just went. And now I am not at work and I am in bed with Joan and it does not seem so unthinkable.

The sunlight finally wakes Joan also, and she rolls onto her side and smiles, still half asleep. There is either nothing or everything to say and so instead we just keep smiling. We smell the cinnamon rising from the confection shop downstairs, a warm current of air that surrounds us. It reminds me that Joan should also be at work, baking with her mother. "Shouldn't you be down there?" I ask her. "You're late for work." She moves on top of me, pins me to the bed. "I could ask you the same thing," she says. I tell her that I don't always have to be at the factory, that it is not my whole life. When I say it, I realize that it's true. I don't have to be there. Joan tells me that she doesn't always have to be downstairs either. "I can be other places too," she says. "I can be upstairs if I like. I can be upstairs all day if I care to." We laugh and watch the sun rise higher and higher through the window.

Later in the afternoon, once Joan and I can no longer put off the rest of the day, we dress and head down the stairs, where Hedy has saved us a few cinnamon rolls. We eat them and then Joan ties on an apron and walks behind the counter. We will see each other again tonight; this we understand without having to say. I go outside and count the steps it takes me to walk somewhere that is not the factory, someplace different.

∘∘
∘∘

It takes five thousand and forty-three steps to walk to the florist, where I purchase a dozen tulips, bright orange. After a bus ride out of the city, it takes me another three thousand and eighty-eight steps to reach the foot of my parents' graves. I place six of the flowers on either side of the single, large tombstone. It is a simple stone, names and dates only. I close my eyes as I run my fingertips over the letters of their names etched into the marble, how perfect each shape feels. I try to think back to what it was like before they were gone, the life we all shared. I think of the four of us in our old house, farther away from the factories and smoke, and pretend we are all there now. We are all at the dinner table, eating, talking, and laughing. But there is nothing else. The memory cannot sustain itself, and it disappears. It gets harder and harder each time to remember my life as anything but the factory, my brother and I alone. It upsets me sometimes, to think that my brother and I have had so little happiness since they died.

I want to be angry with my parents and sometimes I am, but it never lasts. They had no idea what would happen, the strange ways our lives would separate. And it does no good to think that it could have been better or worse or just the same as it is now. There are new things, good things, that I can see for the first time in a while. It makes me smile to finally understand this, that we have only the things we are given, and we must be thankful for them, the tiny, almost imperceptible feeling on our fingertips.

∘∘
∘∘

Here is another way I see it; it is the way I'd like the think it happened, the way that makes sense: My parents, two people who love each other most of the time, ride home on the subway after a fine meal and an average movie. They find an empty subway car and talk, chat back and forth, laugh. They hold hands, fill up the space between them. The subway car gets warmer, the windows fog. My father looks at my mother, red-faced and breathing in rapid bursts. It reminds him of when she had the children. There is a flash, a burst of heat, and my mother looks at my father one last time. My father simply holds on to her hand, pulls himself a little closer to her, to the flash of heat, and covers her body with his. They explode, burn away, and smolder, because sometimes it just makes sense to hold on like that.

∘∘
∘∘

I quit today.

∘∘
∘∘

At the Scrabble factory, a little after two o'clock, I bury my hands in letters and pull up overflowing handfuls, stuffing them into my shoulder bag until tiles leak out from the top and tumble to the floor. I leave the sorting room, tell the supervisor I am going on a bathroom break. He doesn't even look up, couldn't care less about the bag of tiles.

I walk slowly down the corridor until he is out of sight and then I pick up speed, faster and faster until the counter is only a blur, the attendant's orders to stop just a wave of sound that crashes too late. And I am out the door, down the steps, running back to the candy shop, to Joan, though I do not know it yet. Right now, I am just running, one foot in front of the other, and it feels like I will never stop, will never slow down. I am running so fast that the numbers in my head cannot keep up with my feet.

the dead sister handbook: a guide for sensitive boys

VOLUME FIVE (LACONIC METHOD TO NEAR MISSES)

laconic method

Developed by dead sisters in the early 1900s, this method of self-preservation consists of internally processing thoughts and feelings and distilling their essence to one, two, or, at most, three words, which are then made audible. It has since gained immense popularity among all adolescents, but is still most expertly practiced by the dead sister. You find your sister in your room one afternoon. She is curled up in the fetal position on the floor. You ask her if she is okay and she is silent, her eyes closed. Finally, she answers, "I don't know." You ask if you can stay with her. "Whatever," she says. You lie silently beside her until dinner. When you sit down to eat, your mother asks what the two of you have been up to. You are about to tell a complicated, easily uncovered lie, when you hear your sister's voice. "Nothing," she says. "Nothing," you then say, and your sister smiles and nods her approval.

lacrosse

All dead sisters play sports that require sticks—field hockey, ice hockey, etc. (*see also* Sports and Leisure). Dead sisters are aggressive on the field to the point that it is troublesome to sensitive boys. Come game time, the day-to-day boredom of the dead sister, heavy-lidded, gives way to punishing checks, angry shouts after every goal, cups of Gatorade thrown to the ground and stomped on. When you remember your sister, she is red-faced and angry, racing down the field, eager to cause a commotion.

last meal, preparation of

The last meal of the dead sister is always burned (*see also* Arson, Minor and Major Cases of). The dead sister puts something in the oven, goes to watch TV, falls asleep, and awakens to the fire alarm and smoking, charred food. This action provides the sensitive boy with a sensory-triggered memory with which to alter his subsequent life experiences. Smoke precedes the death of something. A girlfriend (*see also* Look-Alikes) burns a pan of snicker-doodles and the smell reminds you of that night, when you ran downstairs to investigate the reason for the insistent beeping of the fire alarm. Your sister is staring into the oven, smoke spilling around her, and she retrieves, with her oven-mitted hand, a single slice of cinnamon toast, burned to black. When she sees you in the doorway of the kitchen, she smiles, takes a bite of the toast, and forces it down. She smiles again and this time her teeth are flecked with black bits of ash and bread. This is one of the last memories you will have of your sister and when your girlfriend reacts disapprovingly to your insistence on eating the burned cookies after she has thrown them in the garbage, you know she will not be your girlfriend for much longer.

legacies (also known as The Dead Sistory)

The family tree of the dead sister is filled with unbranching limbs, categorized by several unusual, untimely deaths occurring exclusively to females. Your great-aunt broke her neck diving into a shallow pond and drowned. Your great-great-grandmother was sleepwalking through the woods beyond her house only seventeen days after the birth of your great-grandfather and was attacked and killed by a bear. Your aunt was smothered in her crib by the family cat before she was a month old. The generational duration of the Dead Sistory is unknown and, by most accounts, unceasing.

lightning, nearly struck by

In the days before death occurs, the heavy deposits of fate inside the dead sister's body serve as a conduit for the discharge of atmospheric electricity. In 27 percent of cases, the dead sister is actually struck by lightning, though never resulting in death. It is raining and your sister was supposed to be home hours ago (*see also* Midnight Equation). You hear the sound of rocks tapping the window and when you look out, there is your sister, soaking wet, her index finger held against her lips. You are to unlock the bathroom window upstairs, which is near the wooden trellis that runs up the wall. You sneak over to the bathroom, unlock the window, and wait. There is a flash of lightning and then a clap of thunder that follows almost instantly. You still cannot see your sister. You think you should go outside, but it is raining and you are afraid to wake your parents. Fifteen minutes later, your sister climbs into the bathroom. She smells of burned sugar. When you ask what happened, she says nothing, walks into her room, and shuts the door. The next morning, you go out to the yard and there is the imprint of her shoes burned into the grass. It will stay there for several weeks after her death, and it will surprise you every time you look out your window.

location of diary

Diary of dead sister (*see also* Papers and Correspondence) is always located in the empty shoebox of her favorite pair of shoes, covered by old quizzes from junior high (*see also* Above-Average Intelligence but Could Have Done So Much Better If She'd Really Applied Herself). This must be found before parents discover its presence. The best time to recover the diary is during the reception that follows the funeral. You will ask to be alone for a little while and everyone will allow this, considering all you've been through. Go into dead sister's room and retrieve diary. Scan quickly for mention of your name, which is rare and, with few exceptions, without incident (*see also* Make Hands). Learn things you had always assumed but had hoped were not true (*see also* Belief That No One Understands Her and She Wishes She Could Go Far Away and Live Her Own Life; Drugs and Alcohol, Abuse of; Sexual Contact with Boys; Sexual Contact with Girls; Suicide, Poetry About). Dispose of diary so no one else can read it.

look-alikes

Sensitive boys will encounter between four and eleven women who resemble the dead sister. Do not, under any circumstances, attempt to talk to these women, follow them down crowded city streets, or pay them money in exchange for sexual favors. Nothing good can come from this.

loss of blood

Dead sisters are obsessed with the creation and preservation of slight, imperceptible wounds. This can be attained by several highly effective methods including: a needle and a composition book; a razor blade and tissue paper; a syringe and glass vials; and a penknife and cotton balls. One night, while your sister is sleeping over at a friend's house (*see also* Sexual Contact with Girls), you rummage through her closet. You find a box filled with daily calendars for the past six years. You pick up the oldest of the calendars, and when you look at January 1, you see a rusty, reddish smudge of what could be blood inside the square for that date. The entire month of January is marked off the same way. The drops of blood in June of that year are slightly darker in such an imperceptible way that you must flip back and forth between the pages of the calendar to be sure. In the most recent calendar, you look at the day's date and see a dark red, almost purple, drop of your sister's blood. You stare so closely at every page, every drop of blood, that even after you have returned the box to its hiding place and gone back to your room, even after you close your eyes for sleep, you can see only dot after dot of red swimming in front of your face. After her death, you try to continue to fill the days of the calendar with your own blood but your fingers begin to ache after three weeks and you have to give up.

loss of child

The sensitive boy secretly believes that his parents, if given the choice, would rather he had died instead of the dead sister. In 80 percent of cases, this is true.

love apples

Food/drink invented by dead sister, derived from soaking peeled tomatoes in a jar of vodka for weeks at a time. Highly toxic and can cause death if consumed in large enough quantities. The alcohol-soaked tomatoes are placed in Ziploc bags and taken to school to be consumed during lunch, which allows dead sister to endure the last half of the school day. After news of sister's death is received, discover the jar of tomatoes and take them to your room. Hide in closet and eat every tomato. This will cause severe illness and an impaired mental state similar to mourning.

magic, lack of

In the 1930s, the Wilmington Method of Sibling Resurrection gained popularity throughout the Deep South and in small pockets of the Midwest. This practice consisted of placing pennies over the entire body of the deceased. The living siblings then would place their hands on the body, warming the coins with their own heat, which transferred to the dead body, causing reanimation. This method worked only when there were eleven or more living siblings participating in the procedure. No living witnesses to the successful practice of this method have ever been located or interviewed. The Tennessee Valley Brother-Sister Exchange and the Thirty-seven Day Lazarus Program have been scientifically discredited and outlawed in all fifty states.

make hands

Term referring to practice performed by siblings, usually a younger brother and older sister less than four years apart, which involves kissing when no one is looking. Originates from when you and your sister, on a camping trip where you shared your own tent, began to kiss each other's hands to practice what you had seen on TV, moving lips softly against the open palm. Soon, this becomes actual kissing and, afterward, when you want to do more of it, you will ask your sister if she wants to go and "make hands." This practice continues until sister determines that this is weird and should be stopped and never mentioned again. Due to unknown chemical reactions in the body, this practice causes at least one of the two parties to die within ten years of initial event.

midnight equation

Mathematical theorem developed in 1975 by feminist mathematician Deborah O'Nan. The age of the dead sister, the established parental curfew, and the exact time of death are plugged into the equation to reveal the exact moment when the dead sister could no longer safely return home, also known as the Clock-Strike Point. The equation generally reveals a difference between the Clock-Strike Point and the time of death to be less than fifteen minutes.

modes of transportation

Death always occurs in relation to a train, airplane, motorcycle, sled, or, most commonly, automobile. In some cases, such as your own sister, it involves two modes of transportation. The car breaks down on tracks or tries to speed across tracks or is simply parked, waiting, on tracks as train approaches. If boyfriend is present (*see also* First Love; Name of Boyfriend), he will always survive. In 30 percent of the cases, boyfriend will be responsible for the accident (*see also* Altercations at Funeral).

muscle spasms

Instinctual response by dead sister to spur body into maturity (*see also* Application of Makeup; Fake ID). Muscles absorb the body's surplus of sugar, nicotine, and pure grain alcohol, and, through intense spasms, speed up the aging process. Packs of ice must be applied weekly to the arms, legs, and chest to prevent overdevelopment.

nail-biter

The sheaths that protect the upper end of the fingers of the dead sister contain small doses of tricyclic antidepressants (*see also* Attempts to Medicate). During stressful situations, the ingestion of the nails potentiates the action of catecholamines and creates a low-level sense of well-being and calm. The body of the dead sister builds up a tolerance to this effect within a few years of development but the instinctual response remains. In particularly bad moments, the dead sister will chew her nails down to the quick and into the flesh, leaving tiny crescents of blood on the papers of tests, the sleeves of her shirts, the skin of those she touches.

name of boyfriend

All boyfriends of dead sisters possess names that can be transposed. Dead sisters date boys named Thomas Alexander or Marcus Benjamin or James Maxwell. Years later, when you try to remember the boyfriend's name, you will switch the order each time. Alexander Thomas.

Benjamin Marcus. This characteristic makes searching for them on the Internet incredibly difficult.

naysaying

Act of refusing all evidence supporting the passing of the dead sister. A technique perfected by sensitive boys, this instinctual response is effective for only up to seventy-two hours after the time of death. The most common acts of naysaying include refusal to answer phone, the locking of doors to bar entrance of parents, the ingestion of substances (*see also* Love Apples), and the temporary loss of hearing and sight (*see also* Sensory Deprivation). The night after her death, you go into your sister's bedroom and take one of her T-shirts from the floor. You place this shirt over one of your pillows and hold it against you as you try to fall back to sleep. The shirt smells faintly of grass and smoke and lavender and everything else that makes up the only remaining elements of your sister. You breathe in the scents and though you cannot sleep, it staves off remembering; it keeps you from crying.

near misses

Dead sisters have two to five incidents before actual death occurs when they could have died—overdoses, car accidents, appendicitis, and on and on and on (*see also* Lightning, Nearly Struck by). You and your sister are in a Ferris wheel at the state fair, sharing cotton candy and watching the lights of the fair brighten and dim with each revolution. As you nearly reach the top of the wheel and the machine grinds to a halt to allow the passengers at the bottom to disembark, the gate to your seat creaks, unlatches, and swings open. There is nothing but you and your sister and the distance between the sky and the earth. Your sister leans forward and peers over the edge. You hold tight to the seat and watch your sister inch closer and closer to the empty space, and though you want to say something, you are quiet. Just before the wheel resumes its movement, your sister finally sits back in the seat, leans her head against the metal grate and gazes at the sky until you reach the bottom. As the wheel stops, your sister steps out of the seat and runs into the murmuring crowd, leaving you alone, your pants wet, asking her to come back, not to leave, but she is already gone.

birds in the house

the men in my family gather at Oak Hall this morning to make birds. They sit in the dining room at an antique oak table and carefully fold their paper cranes. My father and his three brothers fold tiny pieces of paper, squares of yellows and pinks and whites and blues and greens so thin that light passes through them as if they aren't there at all. I watch the brothers' hands, callused and big like sledgehammers, as they struggle not to tear the cranes, not to snap a neck or rip a wing. My uncle Mizell, pressing his oval glasses back onto the bridge of his nose with his thumb, talks about how "Mama always made us do this horseshit. Fold up birds for sick neighbors. Burned my ass to sit there all day and make these things." My father looks up from his bird and scowls at his brother. "Show a little respect, jackass. Fold your son of a bitch birds and we can get this over with." He looks over at me, seated at the far end of the table beside the lawyer, and shakes his head. He does not like being here, I can tell. None of the brothers look happy with the situation, uneasy and wary of their close proximity to one another. They have shown up only because of the will.

Until her death eleven days ago, my grandmother Nobio Collier lived at Oak Hall, a dilapidated plantation in middle Tennessee built by my great-great-great-great-grandfather General Felix Collier of the Confederate Army. The walls are soft from rot and feel like sponge against my fingers. The wood floors have warped slightly, each plank curling up at the ends, like a half smile. It has seen better days, as has the Collier name. After the general died, shot in the back on a failed charge at the Battle of Mill Springs, his five children spent the next forty years fighting over who would get the mansion. The eldest brother was killed, one of the sisters jailed for shooting him, and another sister wandered out into the fields one night and never returned. Finally, the fourth-born, Dwight Collier, a crooked lawyer who had been living in Mason, Tennessee, took up residence at Oak Hall until his death, at which time the property was passed down to his oldest son, a slightly less crooked county executive. Since then, squabbles have erupted from time to time, siblings arguing over who should get what, the money in the family slowly drying up. Folks in Tennessee now say, "The Colliers are bad news with four hundred acres." But Oak Hall is all we have left and so it's not hard to understand why the brothers are gathered here today, taking silent measurements of the house one of them will win, wondering where the TV and sofas will go.

We are all here to settle my grandmother's estate, which consists of the property of Oak Hall and some minor stocks and bonds. There is a small amount of money, but nearly all of that

will pay legal fees and taxes. The brothers are here as partici-
pants in a contest. The lawyer, a thin man with pointy ears who
twirls his pocket watch by its chain, is here to oversee the event.
I am here because, at twelve years old, I am the oldest grandchild, and because my presence was stipulated in her will. The
paper cranes and fans are her ideas as well.

The brothers don't get along. They meet once a year at the
mansion for the family reunion, playing lawn darts and eating
cured ham and drinking whiskey until one of the brothers mentions some ancient grievance. Then we all form a circle around
the combatants and watch them roll around on the grass until
the police show. With my grandmother's passing, they will no
longer keep in touch. They will "see each other in hell," according to my uncle Bit. My grandmother, understanding this rift
between the brothers, this genetic hatred for family that runs
through the Colliers, decided that one brother—only one—will
receive the inheritance. There will be a contest, whose outcome
I will determine, and the winner will take this house and the
other men will return home and live their lives joined in a collective hatred for that one brother.

We will circle around the oak table, a table that was big
enough to seat more than fifty guests in better times, where one
thousand paper cranes will be placed—two hundred and fifty
for each brother. These cranes will then be moved around the
table by the force of four giant fans, positioned at each corner
of the room, until only one paper crane is left on the table. The
owner of that single bird will receive the mansion. However,
before any of this occurs, the brothers must make their cranes,
all one thousand, by hand. It is what my grandmother wanted.
It was her desire, her one last hope, for the brothers to gather
here in the house they once shared, to make birds out of paper

and maybe find something decent in one another that would sustain them. The men in my family are not doing a good job so far.

I want to believe that my grandmother could find no other way to make sure that we all came together than to create such an elaborate game, unavoidable hours around a table. Faced with the finality of the decision, the possibility of losing this house, perhaps she hoped they would come to their senses and make one last attempt at reconciling. And yet, it makes me sad to think that maybe my grandmother, tired from years of unhappiness, had given in to whatever runs in the Collier blood that makes us hurt one another.

There are four hundred and eighty-seven paper cranes scattered across the table and floor of the dining room. The brothers soak their hands in salt water after twenty birds or so, cracking their knuckles and necks and backs and anything else they can get a sound out of. I walk around the room, gathering cranes in a giant wicker basket, checking each bird's left wing for the black marker initials of one of the brothers.

When I bend over to pick up one of the cranes, my uncle Bit flicks my ear. This is the extent of our relationship. He flicks my ear at reunions, twenty, thirty times throughout the day. Sometimes, he'll hide behind trees, wait behind doors, until I come out and he'll flick my ear with a sharp *thwack* and run away, laughing to himself. When I look up, he is concentrating on his crane, trying not to smile. My father says Bit is just plain mean, always unhappy, acting as if God keeps poking him in the back. He is the most well-off of the brothers, working a successful tobacco farm in Robertson County, and though he doesn't need any money or plan to live at the mansion if he wins, he sure as hell doesn't want anyone else to have it. I watch him fold the paper into itself, trying to get the creases right, and then he sets the bird down and shakes the soreness out of his hands. Working in the sun for so many years has left Bit permanently sunburned. The sun has bled into his skin so that he is stained red. When he shakes his hands, it looks like two cardinals flying.

I carry the basket over to the lawyer, seated at the far end of the table, and dump the birds at his feet. The lawyer, a Mr. Callahan from somewhere up north, has long legs, almost obscenely long, and as he tallies each paper crane in his book, they cross and uncross over each other. He is noticeably excited about the contest. He keeps checking his watch, twirling it for a few seconds and then bringing it back to his face. I sit beside him to rest before I start gathering birds again, and I watch the brothers.

My grandmother came to Tennessee from the East. She was not a native Southerner, the first Collier in family history not to hail from below the Mason-Dixon Line. My grandfather Tom Collier met her while in the navy, stationed in Japan just after the Korean War. They hired Japanese teenagers to clean barracks, and he would watch her changing bedsheets, sweeping the floors. She would smile at him as she worked, when he would lift his legs for her to sweep under. Pretty soon he was leaving little gifts for her on his pillow, chocolate and necklaces, a silver lighter. In return, she placed paper objects on the sheets of his bed, origami birds and bears and ships. She liked the way he talked, the slow easy way his words came out, and even though she could hardly understand a word, she knew he said good things, and that was enough.

When his time was up, time to go back to Tennessee and Oak Hall, she came with him. The Collier name slipped even further around town to the point where there wasn't any reason in trying to bring it back to a respectable level. So my grandfather bought a couple liquor stores, and she swept the floors and changed bedsheets in the giant house. The four boys were born, and he sat on the front porch and sipped whiskey and she gradually learned to understand what it was he was saying, learned the things he said weren't as nice as they had been overseas. And this is how my grandmother spent most of her life, figuring out things at Oak Hall weren't as nice as they had been.

My uncle Tetsuya, who will answer only to Soo, though he was named after my grandmother's father, finishes his two hundred and fifty cranes first, and spends the rest of the time wandering around the living room, hovering over the other brothers. He is nervous, chewing a plug of Beech-Nut and spitting into a plastic cup. He walks with me for a while, helps me load the basket with birds, but soon grows tired of this and hovers over Uncle Mizell. Mizell is the biggest of the brothers, nearly three hundred pounds, with arms that look like they could uproot things, trees and telephone poles. He is so big he has to use a machine to help him breathe at night; his third wife is doing five months for unplugging it late one evening. He keeps a towel around his neck to wipe away sweat that trickles down his face and glasses in steady streams. After a few minutes of Soo's beginning to speak and then, thinking better of it, stopping with a quick cough, Mizell spins around and stares him down. "Fairies finish first, that's what I heard." Soo backs up, still coughing words away. Soo runs a near-bankrupt company that makes chocolate shaped like old comic characters, white chocolate Katzenjammer Kids, Li'l Abners made with crisped rice, a nougat-filled Barney Google. He has no money—people apparently don't want to eat beloved comic characters or else don't remember them. Now he spends a lot of time looking over his shoulder, as if a creditor is hiding behind a door. He shoves another tobacco plug into his mouth and sits far away from the other brothers. Mizell finally turns back to his work, tosses another bird on the floor, and mutters, "Burns my ass, all of this."

As the brothers grew older, my grandmother became even more confused, watching these boys of hers run around in the summer months with no shoes or shirts, constantly carrying BB guns and hunting knives. They didn't mind her, and she wasn't sure how to go about making them listen. People in town called them "yellow trash," and this only made the boys pellet their houses even more. My grandfather just drank on the porch and said, "Boys shoot things, honey, that's what they do." They had sunburned skin and fine black hair with rattails. They fought constantly with jeering kids and, when there were no more left to beat up, with one another. I think about my grandmother, sweating in the humid August air and staring out the windows at ragged boys who were half hers kick and bite one another with a ferocity that was nearly joyful. And I think about her staring past the boys, past the mountains on the horizon, and thinking about somewhere else, somewhere far away.

I move beside my father as he finishes the last of the cranes. I cannot help him fold birds—my grandmother's instructions do not allow me to help—so I sit and watch his face, unblinking and staring hard at the paper. It almost looks like concentration, like he is focused on the birds, but I know he isn't; I have seen this look many times in the past year, of staring beyond things in front of him. It reminds me of last year on the cattle farm, of the coolness that should not have been there in late August, the wind coming in from the north. An electric fence was knocked out in a storm, something my father noticed and yet neglected to fix. The cows crossed over into another farmer's patch of crimson clover, where they ate and ate for two days before my father and I saw them grazing in the field. They'd gotten the bloat from the clover, swollen up until there wasn't anywhere for the skin to go but out.

Cows exploded, actually opened up like popped balloons, and they fell over on one side, insides scattered around them. We tried to save the rest, walked them around like crazy to work off the pressure in their stomachs. My father grabbed my Sharp-finger blade and slammed it just above the cow's front quarter, all the way to the hilt, and then pulled it out, trying to open up air passages, but nothing helped. The crimson clover had settled too far inside them and we stood around the field for another two days, cows exploding all around us. Finally my father gave up, went into the house for the Colt .45, and put a bullet between the eyes of every cow still standing until he stood in a cloud of red-tinged dust.

My father used to be a good man, a hard worker. But after the cows, he started to drink more, leased out most of our land to farmers, and kept just enough to get by. He spent long afternoons on the front porch, drinking whiskey splashed with sweet tea, and staring out at that field, at the filled-in ditch where we buried the dead cattle. Around the house, he wouldn't stay in the same room as us anymore, seemed shocked when he happened upon my mom or me, as if he'd forgotten that we existed.

One morning, I woke to find my mother gone and my father out on the porch, drunk. "Where's Mom?" I asked, but he didn't say anything. I asked again and he put his index finger to his lips to quiet me. I sat down beside him and stared out across the field. After an hour, he finally stirred, leaned toward me, and said, "Your mom decided that she needed to be away for a while." I wondered why she hadn't taken me and then, as if he knew what I had been thinking, he said, "I told her that she couldn't take you. I said I wouldn't let you go anywhere. You and me have to stay together, even if neither one of us wants to be here." He started to put his arm around me and then stopped, as if he couldn't understand how to proceed, and then finally, awkwardly, let his arm fall across my shoulders.

If my father wins the mansion, he tells me that he'll fix it up, and then my mother will come back to us; he says that we will have the chance to start over. He will also build a giant wall to keep my uncles out, protecting us from everyone else with our last name. We will sit in the living room and watch football games on a large-screen TV that fills an entire wall. We will dip the winning crane in bronze and keep it on the mantle, where we will stare at it during commercials. I want my mother to come back, though I feel that she has done what my grandmother could never do, has escaped from the Collier name, and I cannot imagine any amount of hoping that could bring her back to us.

There are very few pieces of my grandmother that rubbed off on the brothers. They eat pork rinds wrapped in seaweed. That's about it. They know almost nothing of Japan, of my grandmother's life before she came to Oak Hall. They do not speak a word of Japanese, save for a few curse words that they coaxed out of her to impress other kids at school. They do not remember what all these cranes mean, that a thousand cranes will bring happiness and a long life to those who make them and those they make them for. They remember only the embarrassment of dragging sacks of paper birds down dirt roads to neighbors who were near death, of offering all these folded pieces of colored paper to baffled stares. "I don't want anything to do with your mama's slant-eyed voodoo. Just get those things away from me," they would hear, and the brothers would carry them down to the creek, watch them float in the current before they ducked under the water, all those paper cranes sinking and washing away. And whether they liked it or not, the brothers were half Japanese rednecks in an unhappy family, and it must have been nice to watch something stay above water even for just a few seconds.

When Mizell finishes his last crane, the lawyer and I gather all the cranes, checking the book one last time to make sure we have counted correctly. The brothers mill around the lawyer, jostling one another, watching to see that no one grabs someone else's crane and pockets it.

"Soo, I swear to God I will rip your arm out like a goddamned weed if you take your hand out of your pocket one more time," and Bit looks ready to do it, no longer caring about the contest, just wanting the chance to hit one of his brothers over the head with his own arm.

"I'll place my hands where I damn well please. If you've forgotten last year when you knocked the phone out of my hands and what you got, I'll make you remember pretty damn quick."

I remember that it was my father who knocked the phone away, but I don't say anything, don't remind Soo that my dad knocked out one of his teeth, where it stuck deep in the skin of his fist like a splinter. However, before anyone can remind anyone of anything, the lawyer looks up from the book.

"Gentlemen, the tally is correct and we can get on with this contest. Or, if you have more important business to take care of, we can wait."

birds in the house   65

The brothers grow quiet, step away from the lawyer as if he has drawn a pistol. When the lawyer stands, uncrosses his legs and lifts himself out of his chair, we all hear the sound of paper crinkling, skiffing across the floor. The lawyer lifts one of his feet and sees a crane stuck to his shoe, under his heel, and he sighs, a deep, long sigh that feels like it will go until he has no more breath left in his body when he finishes. He peels the crane off his shoe and holds it up, examines the initials MC on the wing.

"It seems I have miscalculated, or there is a renegade bird here. I have to do a recount now to ensure that each of you has no more or less than two hundred and fifty birds. It will take a few minutes, a half hour maybe. You are free to resume your business, eat or drink or take a short nap if you choose."

The brothers eye one another, no one wanting to be the first to leave the room, to leave their cranes unguarded, but finally my father places his hands on my shoulders and says, "Let's get us some refreshments, Smokey, a little precelebration drink," and with that, all the brothers scatter throughout the house to wait, to look again at what may soon be theirs.

I do not remember much about my grandmother. I saw her only a few times in my life. I remember that even though my father looked different from most of the men in Franklin County, slightly exotic in some way, he still didn't look much like her. Her hair was jet-black even in her old age, her skin yellow-brown. To entertain me, she would let me point to objects in the house and then she would fold paper into that shape, placing the finished product in my hand and waiting for me to pick the next thing. She showed me how to make the cranes and told me the story of their collective power as we filled the floor with what we'd made together, my single crane matching every seven of hers. Once, she took out a photo album and showed me a picture of her and my grandfather in Japan, both wearing kimonos and sitting on a rug. She looked beautiful, her hair pulled into a bun and her face calm and clear. My grandfather looked less comfortable, his kimono puffing at the shoulders, his face twisted to one side, embarrassed, like he had been caught trying on panty hose and a dress. I asked her if she was happy that she'd left, and she told me, "One place as good as another . . . but sometime I think some places may be little better."

My father sits on a stool in the kitchen, swirling the last bits of whiskey left in his glass. His arm is around my shoulder and he is smiling, but I can see his eyes are still far away.

"You okay, Smokey? A lot to take in ain't it? I know it's been a tough year for us, but things gonna get better. I promise you that. Now, here is the thing, Smokey. Maybe I win and maybe not. That's why it's called a contest, but I want you to take this, just to have, just in case."

He reaches down and unrolls his left sock, producing two cranes from the hiding spot; the birds are bright yellow with his initials on the left wings, black ink so dark it looks like it has been branded into the birds. "Where did you get those?" I ask, and he smiles. "I made 'em," he says. "I made 'em when nobody was looking and now I'm giving them to you." He hands them to me, but I shake my head. "We have to play by the rules," I say, and the look on my father's face, the way his eyes turn to slits, makes me feel ashamed, as if I am going against the true nature of things. "These are the new rules I'm giving you," he tells me, the birds now barely touching my chest. "You take these birds and near the end, when things thin out, you get real close to the table and let these birds onto the table. It's not cheating, really. Those birds still have to stay on the table, right?" The plan can end in nothing but failure, the brothers yanking me out of the house and into the yard, accusations, more fighting, but he is my father. He is my family, what's left of it, and though I don't like it, it is what's true. I take the birds from him, carefully fold the wings to meet each other, and slip them into the pocket of my jeans. I look to him, but he doesn't say anything else; he finishes his drink and sits staring out across the kitchen.

The lawyer calls us back into the dining room. The count is correct, everything is ready to go. I begin dumping baskets of paper cranes onto the table, watch them scatter across the oak finish. It is hard to keep them all on the table, takes several tries to get them settled, but when it is done, the lawyer takes one last look at his watch and nods.

Around the table, there are four fans set up, large metal fans that my father says look a lot like "those fans they use on chicken farms. Big son bitches that blow trees down." The fans are all rigged to one control box, whose switch I will flip, starting with the low setting before clicking up to medium and then high. The brothers stand together in a line on one side of the table, staring down at their birds, trying to figure out which ones are theirs, but there are so many, so many colors, that it's impossible to know. Their faces are frozen in tight grimaces, as if the skin around their mouths and eyes is shrinking. When everyone is ready, the lawyer looks at the brothers, looks to me one last time, and says, "Begin."

I click the fans on, listen to them slowly hum. It feels like a slight breeze, and the cranes move slowly around the table, vibrating on the surface like plastic players on an electric football game. Several of the cranes already fall to the ground, tap the wood floors with bent beaks and broken wings. Uncle Bit falls to his knees and picks up the birds, checking each one for initials, yelling out either, "Hell yes, motherfucker!" or "Goddammit all, motherfucker!" depending on what letters he sees. I click the setting to medium, and now the birds are really moving, skittering across the table more quickly than before. The floor is filling up with discarded birds. All the brothers are now on hands and knees, crawling around the table in search of initials, elbowing one another out of the way, pulling hair. Soo kicks out behind him and catches Bit neatly between the eyes, a red print of a loafer forming like a stripe down his face.

More cranes slip off the edge and hover for a few seconds before touching the ground. My father and Uncle Mizell wrestle for a bird, ripping it into tiny shreds in the process. Bit stands up and runs into the hallway for a chair, returning quickly to break it over Soo's back, sending splinters of wood into the air with the paper birds. I click the setting to its final place—on high—and the fans roar, pitch birds around and around the table like things trapped in the center of a tornado. I can hear cursing under the table, the sound of fists smacking against faces and arms and stomachs, yelps of pain. My father is now riding Mizell like a cowboy on a bucking bronc, digging his heels into Mizell's kidneys and screaming, "Get along little doggies." Soo has taken his belt off and cracks it like a bull whip across Bit's back. The lawyer stands in the frame of the door and twirls his watch, his eyes lit up like a man looking through a peephole.

Birds are everywhere, flying to certain death off the edge, hovering two feet over the table, or holding fast to the oak finish. Even cranes that have already fallen to the ground have been picked up again by the fans so that it's hard to tell where anything is anymore, it's just a thick cluster of colored paper birds. The brothers are still rolling around on the floor, covered in thin, bright red paper cuts. They occasionally stop pummeling one another to look up at the table and shout words of encouragement. Mizell's head pops up like a groundhog and he screams, "Hold on you sons of bitches, hold on." And I lean forward, hands almost touching the table, and watch this swirling mist of colors, of delicate paper cranes hovering, hanging, flying in the air. I sometimes have to hold my hands over my face to block cranes crashing into my head. The fans put out so much wind that it feels like a monsoon, like the whole house is going to lift off the ground and touch down somewhere else. The brothers are bleeding and bruised and screaming profanity like holy men speaking in tongues.

The birds are flying, if only for a brief moment, and I watch a rainbow of cranes fly around the room, dip and loop and dive in the air. I reach into my pocket, feel the two cranes against my fingertips, but I can't release them. I look at my father, his shirt ripped and his back scratched red with jagged lines, and he is crawling across the ground while a swarm of birds shoot past him so quickly that it seems as if they are attacking him. I have seen my father fight with his brothers before, have grown accustomed to the sight of his broken fingers, swollen face, and busted lip, still smiling. But today, in the midst of these cranes, it seems especially ugly, makes me sad that my father cannot share this moment with me. I am afraid of what will happen if we do not win this house, but it is even harder to imagine my father and I alone in all of these rooms, filled with so much unhappiness.

The cranes are still flying around the room, and, even though I won't cheat, I can't deny these birds in my hands the chance to move with the rest. I open my hands and let them take to the air, watch them lift out of my grasp like baby birds flying for the first time, and their yellow shade mixes with the swirl of colored birds above me. And it is beautiful, to watch these things, these tiny creatures move so quickly through the air, to watch them pick up speed and soar from the table like airplanes lifting off a runway. They take to the air and fly away, out windows, through the hallway, into deep parts of the house where they will never be found.

And then it happens—the crane. All the brothers stop mid-punch, release chokeholds. They remain on their knees, look up at the table with swollen eyes wide. The final crane, bright red, has been caught perfectly between the four fans, equidistant from each one, and this crane catches the wind and soars into the air, raises off the table, and still climbs higher.

The brothers are motionless, cannot even curse in their wonder. There is no way to make out the initials. The crane hovers four feet above the table, caught between the fans so that it hovers, levitates without moving. I think it is amazing, seeing something so beautiful flying inside the walls of Oak Hall. And for one moment it is wonderful to watch this single paper crane hang in the air like a prayer, like hope, like a single breath.

But when I look over at the brothers, on hands and knees as if praying, I know that all they can see is the mansion, the house that one of them will have when this bird touches down. They jab elbows into ribs, ball their hands into tight fists, and press the weight of their bodies into one another. They want only one thing, for that bird to fall, to drift beneath the current of wind. They wait for the crane to dive back to the table, where they will rip it open, tear it apart for the answer, while I watch it hover, want only for it to stay up there forever. The brothers are ready, watching it begin to wobble and lose flight.

And just before it touches down, before the four brothers slam into one another to place their hands upon the paper crane, I think about my grandmother and hope that she is somewhere far away, somewhere that even birds cannot reach, and I hope that she is happy.

mortal kombat

there are two boys in the library, hiding in the A/V room. In this small, windowless room, there are three film projectors, four TVs and VCRs, seven overhead machines, and these two boys. They sit on the floor, their lunch around them, and run through random information as quickly as they can, things no one else knows.

They are academic athletes, Quiz Bowl teammates, and they are also, of course, very unpopular. Their sole extracurricular activity involves traveling all over the state and competing against other very unpopular teenagers, answering random academic questions. They don't begrudge this fact; they are now juniors and nearly three years of this has left them resigned to their fate. They do not fit correctly into the spaces available to them.

Their comics are not bagged and backboarded, alphabetically arranged. They like drugs but are too afraid of getting caught to mention this to anyone else. If they enjoyed role-playing games, like Dungeons & Dragons, they would pretend that they wore cloaks of invisibility that kept others from noticing them, but they do not like Dungeons & Dragons, find it embarrassing to pretend. And though people might guess, if they cared enough to venture a guess, that they are smart, their considerable knowledge is esoteric and not reflected in their grades, which are passing but not spectacular. Their few forays into expanding their group, of finding other friends, has been met by awkwardness and immediate regret. They are alone in the world, in the school, in this tiny room, but they are together and that helps; they make each other possible.

They no longer feel weird about the fact that they skip lunch with all the other students in order to study in the library. They do not care that even the other two Quiz Bowl members, the valedictorian and his girlfriend, think that they are strange. They could be happier, and they could easily tell you the specific ways they could be happier, but they know it probably won't happen. They know lots of things, and what they don't know, they will learn.

At first glance, the boys seem almost identical: baggy clothes with pictures of comic book characters or names of obscure bands on them, jittery, patches of acne, very pale. But looking closer, there are enough differences.

Wynn is newly tall from a growth spurt this summer, still awkward in his changing body. Until this year, he played junior varsity soccer, but he has grown bored with it, no longer understands his former teammates' enthusiasm. His body is still muscular from the necessities of the sport, a byproduct that he is happy about. His hair, which he does not bother to comb, is curly, spiraling out in all directions.

Scotty is shorter, freckled, still pudgy with baby fat. He is waiting for puberty to fully kick in and now suspects, or fears, that it will not happen at all. His hair hangs down in his face, obscuring his eyes so that when he looks up at someone, he can't really see the person at all. He likes it this way.

They spit questions and answers back and forth so quickly that it sounds like another language. Wynn is asking Scotty about 1989 Oscar winners, and, in return, he is answering questions regarding political embarrassments. They have their backs placed firmly against each other, their spines neatly aligned, and sit cross-legged, their eyes focused on opposite walls. They go.

"Best costume design."

"*Henry the Fifth*. Watergate."

"Nixon. Supporting actress."

"Brenda Fricker, *My Left Foot*. Only president to be impeached."

"Andrew Johnson. Honorary Oscar for achievement in film."

"Oh, that Japanese guy. Mifune."

"Kurosawa."

"Shit. Chappaquiddick."

"Ted Kennedy."

"No, Edward Kennedy."

"Same person."

"Really?"

"Yeah. Ted is Edward."

And then there is silence while they drink from their juice boxes and eat crackers. They move on to African countries and their capitals, planets and their discoverers, presidents and order of death. The napes of their necks rub against each other, close cut and prickly. The room isn't air-conditioned and smells sour, like dust and old oranges. They stop questioning each other for a few minutes, let their minds rest.

It is a Friday, and after school they are going to watch movies, play video games, get high. They have not been invited to any parties, and would feel strange going to one even if asked. This is their routine, and to stray from it seems to be asking for trouble. They argue over which movies to rent, discuss the possibilities of purchasing weed or stealing some Valium from the medicine cabinet of Wynn's aunt, agree for the uncountable time that school sucks, that this whole place sucks, and then there is nothing left to say. It is time to return to their classes; lunch has ended.

They press their backs even harder against each other and attempt to stand without using their hands. Just before they gain their footing, Scotty slips and tumbles to the floor, pulling Wynn down with him. Wynn slams his elbow on the floor and the pain shoots all the way from his arm to the base of his head. He grabs Scotty, yells, "Fucker," and then they are lying on the floor, tangled up. They are grinning, shoving each other, and trying to stand. Then they are kissing, clicking teeth in the force and quickness of their decision. It makes them pull back for a second, the strange metallic sound of their teeth hitting. Their faces are completely unlined, expressionless.

It is simple and awkward at the same time, the way they proceed. There is only the quickness of movement, the instinctive responses of the body. It feels like fighting; that is what runs through both of their minds. It lasts all of two minutes, maybe less. When it is over they are sweating and shirtless, skin burned red in the shape of handprints, backing away from each other in small, careful steps.

When school lets out, they avoid each other in the parking lot, keep their distance.

Wynn goes home and tells his mother that he doesn't feel well. He is pale, but hot to the touch. And it is the weekend, so she lets him off the hook. He crawls into bed, waits for sleep, and hopes that he will dream of nothing, a complete blank.

Scotty steals a porn magazine from his father's closet, women who are barely legal but still older than Scotty. He doesn't read it immediately, simply keeps it under his mattress, which calms him. That night, when his body stiffens and he grips himself, he pulls out the magazine and flips through the pages. The ease of this, how familiar it is, makes him forget what happened with Wynn. When he comes, there is nothing special about it, easily forgotten, and he falls asleep with the magazine still on the bed.

Both boys sleep late on Saturday, notice the sunlight coming in through the windows, but don't move. They wake with erections and try to ignore them.

Finally, Scotty gets out of bed, returns the magazine to his father's closet, and goes outside to rake the leaves, his one weekend chore. As he arranges the leaves in little piles all over the yard, he keeps thinking about Wynn, the A/V room. He tries to remember if he's ever considered the possibility of it before, wonders if Wynn has. He has no other friends. His prospects for a girlfriend seem slim. What he has is Wynn. They hang out all the time, study together, sleep over. Scotty knows it is less than what he wants, that he would be happier with Kallie Michaelson and the curves of her body, but this could work. The thought of yesterday, him and Wynn and the force of their movements, seems less and less frightening. He is not gay, at least he doesn't think so, but he could be for now. He finishes raking the leaves and walks over to Wynn's house, though he has no idea what he will say or do when he gets there.

Wynn still lies in bed, refuses to move. He feels sick enough now that the lie he originally told seems true. When the doorbell rings, he pulls the sheets up to his chin to cover himself, bashful, and instantly feels stupid. He knows it is Scotty. He listens to his mom tell Scotty that he isn't feeling well, is still asleep. Once Scotty leaves, his mother comes into his room, tells him about his friend, and then leaves to take his sister to dance class. He is alone in the house, and suddenly he feels hungry for the first time in a while. He reaches into the drawer of his nightstand and eats a handful of PEZ candy. He thinks about going downstairs and making a sandwich when he hears the *tock-tock* sound of something bouncing off the window in his room.

He walks over to the window and sees Scotty, lobbing little pebbles up at him. Wynn crouches down beneath the window and fumbles to put on a pair of pants, a shirt. He lifts the window and Scotty calls, "Can you come down for a second? Or do you want me to come up?" The easy way that Scotty says this makes Wynn flush red, angry and embarrassed at the same time. Wynn lifts the window a little more. "No," he says. "I'm sick." Scotty throws another pebble and Wynn pulls away from the window. "Come down," Scotty says, "I know you aren't sick." Wynn grabs a tennis ball off the floor and throws it out the window, which Scotty dodges easily. "I'm sick," he says again. "I'll see you on Monday." He watches Scotty shrug his shoulders and begin to walk away. "You feel weird?" Scotty asks Wynn, though it sounds less like a question and more like a statement of fact. "Yeah," Wynn says and then closes the window.

Sunday night, neither of them can sleep. They are nervous about what might happen tomorrow, or what might not. They both started breaking out this morning, new patterns of acne. Whatever happens, no matter how it ends up, both of them know that it will only make them more awkward and weird, an easier target for the people who make fun of them. Both wish they were eighteen and out of high school, believing without proof that life cannot get much worse.

Presidential assassination attempts. Nobel Prize winners. NBA record holders. Wynn treats all of these subjects with such attention, such focus, that it is almost as if Scotty is not in the room with him. Almost. They sit facing each other today, careful not to touch. Encyclopedias, World Almanacs, and the *Guinness Book of World Records* are spread out in front of them, providing a boundary that separates them. It is easy enough to ask these questions, just as easy to answer them, but Wynn knows there are other things to talk about, senses that Scotty wants to address them. He looks across the line of books and notices Scotty's eyes, barely hidden by the bangs that hang down almost to his nose, darting back and forth between the encyclopedia in his lap and Wynn, expectant. So Wynn keeps spouting trivia.

And when there are no other questions left to ask, or no more time left to ask them, Wynn feels his neck muscles tense. Scotty seems to lean forward, past the opened books, and Wynn pulls back farther. "Um . . . so are you ready to get Mortal Kombat?" he asks Scotty, who slumps back down and smiles. Perhaps he is grateful for the diversion as well. "Oh yeah," he responds, "I even found an advance cheat so we can perform the fatalities." And they spend the rest of the lunch hour this way, talking about punches, kicks, and mutilation in a way that makes their voices crack.

Mortal Kombat is what they have both been saving up their allowances for months in order to buy. They have spent buckets of quarters at the arcade already, playing this fighting game with splatters of blood, realistic violence, spines ripped out of the tops of heads. It makes other video games seem silly, juvenile. And next week, when it is finally released for home entertainment consoles, they will have it. The prospect of it, of playing it in their own houses, keeps them happy when there are many reasons not to be. And, even better, it is so easy to talk about that they smile nervously here in the A/V room, talk about the different characters and moves and blowing flames out of their mouths and burning opponents to a crisp.

Scotty balls up a piece of notebook paper, presses the base of his palms together so his hands look like an open mouth, and, like the character Sub-Zero who shoots bolts of ice, flings it at Wynn. It hits Wynn in the face, and he immediately halts his actions, muffling laughter, encased in ice. Scotty kicks books out of his way and moves closer to Wynn, who is not smiling anymore but still frozen. Scotty, on hands and knees, looks directly at Wynn, inches away from him. He waits, gives Wynn the chance to back away, to unfreeze, and when he doesn't, he kisses him. This time it's softer and less hurried. Afterward, before either of them can speak, Scotty scrambles out of the room without looking back. The door closes but Wynn still doesn't move. He is still frozen, though he feels flush, realizes how strange it is that he could melt ice just by touching it to his skin.

That night, Scotty walks around the building where he works, emptying trashcans, mopping the floor, and cleaning the urinals. On Monday through Thursday nights, he works as the janitor for his uncle's realty firm. It is an easy enough job, solitary, and he can listen to music on the company PA system. He has Joy Division turned up loud as he cleans the panes of the glass doors, one of his last jobs before he can leave. The music is depressing in its lyrics but undermined by a bouncing bass line, a strange mixture of doom and dancing. He wipes the glass in time to the beat, nodding his head so that his bangs tap his forehead. As he cleans, he notices a pair of headlights pull up in the parking lot. The presence of another person makes him immediately stop moving, embarrassed by the nearly imperceptible head bobbing that he defines as dancing. It is Wynn's car. He walks up to the door, so that only the glass is between them. Wynn holds up some new comic books, wriggles a joint between his fingers, and points at the handle of the door. Scotty lets him in.

They smoke in the break room, flip through the comics, and pass the joint back and forth without saying much of anything. By the time the joint is finished, they have each read the two comic books, and though the Joy Division CD has ended and the silence is noticeable, neither can think of anything to say. To talk about the comic books they just read doesn't enter their minds. Or what happened earlier today. Or why Wynn is here when he almost never comes over when Scotty is working. Instead they look through the company minifridge and grab the only things in it, diet soda and cottage cheese. Finally, their curfews fast approaching, they get ready to leave.

Scotty sweeps the ashes off the table and into his open hand, throws out the soda cans. And all that is left is to turn out the lights and empty the dirty water in the mop bucket, a task he always saves until last. He goes to the janitor's closet to get the bucket, and Wynn follows behind him. Scotty pulls the chain to light up the tiny closet and they are both so close, almost touching in the cramped space. Wynn only stands there, will not stop staring at Scotty, who cannot figure out how to proceed. It seems too ridiculous, too embarrassing.

Instead, he kneels down, reaches into the bucket, and tosses a handful of blackish water at Wynn, who is too close to dodge it. Wynn shouts and kicks over the bucket so they are both standing in the puddle, watching it spill out from the door and into the hallway. It smells like rubber for some reason, and makes their sneakers squeak when they walk awkwardly out into the hall. "Jerk," Scotty says and then reaches for the mop to clean the hallway again. Wynn knocks the mop out of his reach and pushes him against the wall, keeps smacking Scotty's hand away as he continues to reach for something. And then it starts again. Scotty rubs his hand against the crotch of Wynn's jeans, burning his palm on the fabric until the skin is bright red. Scotty has done things with a few girls, back in grade school, and it seems almost the same, touching and moving until something feels good. He sneaks his tongue into Wynn's mouth, which Wynn tries to spit out. Scotty does it again and tastes the staleness of pot. As they slump to the floor, their pants get undone, shirts off, and, as they move, the water that has pooled around them slaps at their arms and legs. Wynn's elbow smacks Scotty in the face, but neither of them notices. They are both so close. And then the particulars race through their minds. It is one thing to kiss some guy, even to touch his dick, but it is another thing to come because of him.

For Wynn, it is about crossing a line that he does not know enough about to think that he can cross back. He has never been with another person: no girls, no games of doctor behind the shed. This is it and he is close and he can't pretend this doesn't feel good, but suddenly he stops, he can't keep going. "Wait," he says, "wait," and grips Scotty's wrist to stop him. He stands up, puts on his damp clothes, and runs out to his car. He lies flat in the back seat and prays that Scotty will not come out. He realizes that he is still hard, and he starts to stroke himself, imagines him and Scotty with a girl whose specifics he cannot conjure up. She is a girl, at least that much, and that is all he can figure before he comes, safe. He peers over the seat and wonders if Scotty is going to come look for him, if he should wait.

Scotty walks into the bathroom and notices that he is still wearing his sneakers, naked except for them. He stands in front of a urinal and jerks himself off. In the mirror above the sinks, he notices the puffy redness around his right eye, from Wynn's elbow. It stings to the touch, but he keeps lightly brushing his finger over the spot. Finally, he dresses, mops up the water in the hallway, and walks out to his car. Wynn is gone.

That night, both boys replay the events in their heads. It is fascinating and alarming at the same time, how quickly things can go. They try to further the moment, take it as far as it can go, but their imaginations fail them. They are left only with what has happened, the imprint each has left on the other's body, and they wait for tomorrow without dread or anticipation, only curiosity as to how it can continue.

The next day, Wynn wears his favorite T-shirt, the one with a long set of graphics that indicate a series of control moves "UP-UP-DOWN-DOWN-LEFT-RIGHT-LEFT-RIGHT-B-A-START," which is a video game code. Every time that he wears it, he has this tiny wish that someone will ask him what it means, will show interest. But no one ever does. They either already know, or more likely, don't give a shit. He arrives in the library before Scotty, picks up the key for the A/V room from the librarian, who allows their surreptitious studying without encouraging it, and begins choosing books for their quizzes, several encyclopedias and a sports almanac. He has a feeling of expectancy, a rudimentary belief that things can only escalate in this kind of situation. He suspects the books he has gathered will not be used today, but this has only made him more careful in the choosing.

They start with easy questions, their favorites. Heisman Trophy winners. Famous explorers and their discoveries. Matching poets to famous lines. They answer without thinking, each responding before the other has finished speaking. There are harder questions to ask. Do you want to? Is it okay? Should we? Maybe. Maybe. Okay. It gets easier after that.

Wynn keeps saying, "Quiet, we have to be quiet." They keep their clothes on, but their pants are so baggy, it is easy to slip their hands underneath. Scotty works his hand up and down, his face resting against Wynn's shoulder, and when it is finished, Wynn makes a strangled, whining sound like he wants to say something he can't put into words. Scotty rolls onto his back and Wynn moves on top of him. He starts to pull up his shirt when the door creaks, the knob tries to turn.

The door is locked but there is still the quick rush of fear, the worst thing that could happen. Wynn recoils, feels his face flush with anger, and punches Scotty in the ribs. It is so fast that neither boy knows what has happened. Scotty doesn't cry out, though he can feel the sharp pain with each breath. He tries to pull his shirt back down and then they hear the librarian tell them through the door that she needs to get a TV/VCR unit for one of the history classes. Wynn is already flipping books open, shoving crackers in his mouth, pulling his shirt as far down as it will go. He is creating the scene, preparing their alibi. Scotty is still on the ground, looking up at Wynn, who is hissing, almost silent, "Get up. Get up, you fucker. Hurry." He stands, unsteady, while Wynn opens the door.

The librarian asks nothing, doesn't suspect a thing, or, if she does, doesn't reveal anything. She simply wheels the cart out of the room, shuts the door, and leaves Wynn and Scotty alone in the room again, so scared that they have no idea what to do now. Scotty crouches on the floor, breathing softly and wincing. Wynn feels his heart beating in his chest and cannot focus his thoughts, can hardly remember hitting Scotty. His mouth opens, but there is no sound. He kneels down and places his hand on Scotty's face, Wynn's fingers tracing the bones around his friend's eyes. Scotty cannot look at Wynn just yet, embarrassed by the soft whimpers he now makes, and hunches over one of the books, still holding his ribs. Finally, Wynn removes his hand from Scotty's face and walks to a corner of the room with one of the books. They sit in silence, afraid to move, and wait for the lunch period to end. Scotty does not ask Wynn any more questions, simply absorbs what has happened, amazed at what he's never even thought of before.

After school, Wynn drives around aimlessly for an hour with the radio off. He cannot keep doing this. He knows it may not be true, but he believes that he is better than what is happening. He feels that he can still turn things around if he wants. He could rejoin the soccer team, eat lunch in the cafeteria, make new friends. And even if none of this happens, he can still stop messing around with Scotty. He has to, feels that to keep going like this will only end with something terrible happening. He thinks about Scotty's hand on him, jerking him off, and then remembers punching him. He feels ashamed about both things. Wynn wants to go back to how it was before, both of them unhappy, unpopular, unable to change. He finally pulls into his driveway as the sun begins to set and notices Scotty sitting on the curb, his knees pulled up to his chest, waiting.

There is little to say, but even that is difficult for Scotty to draw out of Wynn. He has been here since school let out, reading comics, watching cars drive by. Wynn's mother offered him a drink, asked him inside, but he wanted to wait out here, to be the first thing Wynn saw. And now that they are in public, things are awkward. Scotty asks Wynn if he wants to come over to his house to talk, but Wynn says no, he is done. He doesn't want to do it anymore. "You do," Scotty insists.

Wynn tells him that he isn't going to study in the A/V room anymore, wants to be alone for a few weeks. Scotty puts his hand on Wynn's shoulder but he shrugs it off, jerks away. "Not out here," Wynn says, and then corrects himself, "not anywhere." Scotty feels on the verge of crying, but the thought of Wynn seeing him cry is too embarrassing. He picks up his backpack and stands, grimacing at the dull pain in his side. He pulls up his shirt and shows Wynn the bruise. "You hurt me," Scotty says. Wynn won't look at him, stares at his hands, but says, "I'm sorry."

For the next few days, they are apart. Scotty stays in the A/V room but he does not read. He just sits there, waits for Wynn, even though he never shows up. Wynn eats in the cafeteria but the room feels too big, so much noise. He sits at a table with some of his old teammates from the soccer team. When he asks if he can sit with them, they seem to have trouble remembering him for a few seconds before one of them finally nods toward an empty seat, and he feels even more ridiculous, but he refuses to seek out Scotty, to go to the A/V room, where he knows his friend is waiting. In his head, while the boys at the table talk about baseball players that Wynn has never heard of, he runs through the battles of the Civil War until it is time to go back to class. During the two classes that they share, Scotty stares at the back of Wynn's neck, hoping that Wynn will answer a question so he can hear his voice. One night, Wynn thinks he hears something tapping against the window of his room, but when he looks outside he can't see anything. He raises the window and calls out, almost whispering, "Scotty?" No one answers, even when he asks again.

A single thing breaks up the sameness of these days, Mortal Kombat. It finally arrives in stores and each of them waits in line for over two hours to buy a copy. Wynn drives three towns over to avoid running into Scotty, driving the entire way back home with one hand on the wheel and the other clutching the game. They hunker down in their rooms, lights off, gripping controllers, intent. They have different game systems, and Wynn's brand, bowing to parental and governmental concerns, will play only a censored version of the game. No blood. No heads exploding from electrocution. Not nearly as much fun. He knows that Scotty has the bloody version, all the good things, but still he will not call him. He punches and kicks, sweat instead of blood flying off his opponents, and tells himself that this is just as good. He is happy enough.

Sometimes Scotty pretends that the person he is fighting in Mortal Kombat is Wynn. When he punches the character's head right off its body, he smiles for a second and then immediately feels bad. One night, he calls Eileen Brenner, a girl he knew slightly in junior high. They danced a single song at a Spring Fling Dance. She doesn't seem to remember him but still he asks her if she would like to see a movie sometime. She says that she is kind of seeing someone, not seriously, but she can't do anything with Scotty. He is slightly relieved, even thanks her, and hangs up. He is sure that will get around school, more evidence of his awkwardness. He won't call Wynn, has promised himself that, but he finds that much of his time is spent waiting for

Wynn, hoping he will call. He knows that Wynn's version of the game is second-rate. He hopes that blood and severed heads and people impaled on sharp spikes will make Wynn want to be near him.

More days pass and Wynn is restless. He hardly even plays Mortal Kombat now. Without the blood, it seems silly, like Saturday morning cartoons. He doesn't sit with Scotty in the A/V room anymore. He doesn't see Scotty at all anymore. He just sits in his room, reads comic books, smokes pot when his mother and sister are gone, and tries not to do anything at all. Occasionally, the thought of Scotty pops into his head, like a random fact from an encyclopedia. It is troubling and yet reassuring, the way his mind can retain information, can remember. At night, when he jerks off, he thinks of absolutely nothing, merely performs the necessary task, and finishes. Finally, for no reason that he can think of, to separate this from another day, he picks up the phone and calls Scotty. Scotty answers on the first ring and, before Wynn can finish his stuttered greeting, says, "Come over."

Scotty waits on the street in front of his house until he sees Wynn walking up the sidewalk. He meets him and asks Wynn if he wants to go for a walk, just to talk. Wynn shakes his head. "I just want to play the game," he says, "that's all." Scotty is fine with this, is tentative and nervous around Wynn at the moment, and welcomes the familiarity of video games. They go inside, past Scotty's parents, who nod silently at Wynn, completely unaware that he hasn't been around lately. Scotty shuts the door to his room and sits close to Wynn, hands him a controller. And then, silently, they play.

There is blood, waves of it coming off the characters like a pattern of birds flying away. Punches, kicks, high kicks, low kicks, uppercuts, jumping punches, ice blasts, laser blasts, fly-ing hooks. The only sound in the room is the ominous music of the game, the deep voice of the unseen announcer, who starts each match with the single word, *FIGHT!* Wynn and Scotty don't talk; the only sound between them is the rapid-fire *tap-tap-tap* of their fingers on the controllers. They are equally matched, fights going back and forth. Pretty soon, after one ending move where Wynn knocks Scotty off the bridge and into the pit of spikes, both boys laugh. It is easy and predictable, the way friends come back to each other.

After a while, Wynn begins to develop a strategy. He jumps back and forth in rapid succession, landing multiple kicks and punches until he wins. He keeps beating Scotty, four in a row, five in a row, six in a row. Each time, while Scotty's character wobbles unsteadily at the end, beaten, the announcer cries out, FINISH HIM! And Wynn calmly punches the buttons, and they watch his character reduce Scotty's to a skeleton of ashes. It starts to get on Scotty's nerves. "That's a chickenshit way to win," he mutters, but Wynn just laughs and they keep playing. Scotty wishes he had picked a better character than Kano, some stupid cyborg whose reach is too short, his sweeping kicks un-able to cover any ground. But he won't choose another charac-ter until he wins just once; the improbability of this happening makes Scotty angrier with every loss.

Wynn knows that he is aggravating Scotty but cannot stop. He wants to keep winning. Each time, he laughs softly, feels happy. He thinks that he can beat Scotty into submission, that they can go back to how it was before if he can just make Scotty give up. He keeps punching, kicking, bouncing back and forth. "You give up?" Wynn asks, but Scotty doesn't say a word, just keeps tapping his controller.

It's the eleventh straight loss, and now Scotty is pissed. He hates the way Wynn keeps bouncing around, won't stay and fight. Normally, Wynn would cut it out and they could go back to the old way of fighting, but not tonight. Scotty feels that he is being made fun of, the way Wynn has come over here, refusing to talk about the things that matter, and keeps beating Scotty to a pulp. For the eleventh time in a row, he watches himself reduced to cinders, his body collapsing. He looks over at Wynn, who is smiling. "That's a faggot way to fight," Scotty says and watches the muscles in Wynn's neck tighten. "What did you say?" Wynn asks him. "A faggot would fight like that," Scotty says again, and smiles, just barely. Match number twelve begins and Scotty thinks that this is it, that he can win, that he can have what he wants.

Scotty wins the first round. Wynn makes too many mistakes and walks right into Scotty's punches and kicks. In the second round, he recovers enough to squeak out a victory, throwing a flying hook and landing an uppercut at the last minute to even the score. Neither boy says anything or looks away from the screen during the final round. It is a flurry of punching, back and forth. Neither of them backs away, each simply takes what the other has to give and hopes he will last. Finally, a quick block, a change of momentum, and Scotty sweep kicks Wynn to the ground, beaten. The voice returns: FINISH HIM! Scotty looks over at Wynn, who will not meet his eyes. He waits for Wynn to look at him but is aware that time is running out before the game will end itself. Finally he punches in the combination and they both watch the screen as Scotty walks over to Wynn and reaches into his chest, pulls out his heart. "There," Scotty says finally, and kisses Wynn, almost biting his lip.

Wynn feels Scotty's mouth against his, the roughness of how

their lips meet. He kisses him back and then, without a sound, smashes his fist against Scotty's jaw, knocks his friend to the ground. Scotty inches away, touching his hand to his mouth, which is now bleeding. "Fuck you," Scotty says, and spits a wad of saliva and blood at Wynn. Wynn thinks to apologize, is shocked by the sight of his friend, but instead he says, "Fuck you too," and walks out of the room. He runs down the stairs, out of the house, and doesn't stop until he can no longer see Scotty's house, is completely alone. He looks back in the direction of Scotty's house and feels like he is going to cry. Scotty is his only friend, and now he has no friends, not one. He thinks about the kiss and then the punch and feels his hands ball into fists again. He wants to scream. He paces in a tight circle, unsure of where to go. He looks over his shoulder and starts to walk, then freezes. There is a smear of blood on his forearm, Scotty's blood, and he rubs it into his skin until it disappears. He has no idea what to do, or what he is capable of doing. He just stands there, in the street, and waits for something to make sense.

Scotty takes a sock off the floor and presses it tight against his mouth. The bleeding has almost stopped. On the screen, because of the inactivity of the players, the computer has taken over the fighting, controlling both characters. He watches the fighting for a few minutes, the back and forth, and then turns off the game. The room is completely dark now. He crawls over to his window and looks out onto the street. He cannot see Wynn, assumes that he is far away. He slumps down under the window, presses his back tight against the wall. He is crying but he can't feel it. He doesn't know what else to do and so he studies, alone. He names every president. From George Washington on down the line. Then in alphabetical order. Then by number of terms. Then he breaks them down by party affiliations. There are more permutations, but he doesn't care. All he wants to know is if Wynn will come back tonight and he is certain that he will learn soon enough, that he will finally have the answer.

tunneling to the
center of the earth

first of all, we were never tunneling to the center of the earth. I mean, we're not stupid. We knew we couldn't get to it with the materials we had. The psychiatrist that Mom and Dad hired to talk to me is responsible for the whole *Journey to the Center of the Earth* thing because, to him, what we were actually doing wasn't as exciting. In fact, I don't think he ever fully understood what we were doing. I don't think we really understood it either. We were just digging.

It started last summer. The three of us, Hunter, Amy, and myself, had just graduated from college with meaningless degrees, things like Gender Studies and Canadian History and Morse Code. We had devoted our academic careers to things we couldn't seem to find applicability to the world we were now in. We never really thought about it when we were in school, reading about gender and Canadians and Samuel Morse. We never realized that we were supposed to be preparing ourselves for future lives, self-sustainable lives with jobs and all the other things like family cars and magazine subscriptions. And so I think it was that kind of disconnection from what we were expected to do that made us get out the shovels. It's the only reason I can figure.

We had just been sitting around in my room at my parent's house since graduation. We still wore our graduation caps, would twirl the tassels like strands of hair as we watched TV or played cards or smoked cheap pot that Amy's brother sold us. My mother would leave the want ads outside the door of my room and that's where I left them, too. "Maybe you could teach Morse code to kids at the elementary school," she told me one morning as we ate breakfast. And sure, I would have loved to teach kids Morse code, to tap my finger onto their tiny palms and explain the words being formed on their hands. But schools can hardly afford to teach real languages like Spanish and French.

Besides, people want to know how to say only two things: "I love you" and "SOS." They wanted to know a romantic code and then tap it out on their lover's naked body and spend the night a little less lonely. So at parties I was always tapping out the same things, showing drunk people the correct timing, the pauses necessary to say the words. But even then it didn't matter. They would tap whatever they wanted, correct or not, and their lover would be happy. And if they were in a situation where they actually had to resort to using Morse code for help, well, they were not going to get it. They were going to die.

∎∎

None of us came up with the idea on our own that morning. It just sort of hit us all simultaneously. You spend enough time

tunneling to the center of the earth

with someone, you start to think in sync with them, and at this moment we all just thought the same thing: *We should dig, get underground.* So we did.

We went to the garage and grabbed all the shovels and digging tools we could find. Hunter took the posthole digger, for the initial opening, plus another shovel for once we got started. I had a new shovel, with a perfect, unblemished silver spade and a lacquered handle. I also took one of those shovels with the pointed spade, to break through the rocks or tree roots that we'd likely come across. Amy wore two garden trowels on her hips like a gunslinger, for the intricate digging and shaping along the sides of the hole. She also filled one of her pockets with spoons from the kitchen, just in case.

We stepped outside the garage with purpose, weighed down with our tools, and walked into the backyard. My mother was washing dishes in the kitchen and slid open the window. "What are you kids doing?" she asked us. I told her that we were going to dig a hole. She asked us to stay away from her tulip garden and we did, picked a spot in the far corner of the yard and started digging.

We worked day and night that first week, burrowing down a good twelve feet into the earth, expanding the hole so that all three of us would fit at the same time. We took our lunch breaks back on the surface, where my mother would bring us sandwiches and chips and lemonade. We liked to lie on our stomachs and eat our food, staring down at the hole we'd made. We'd gotten down far enough to where we were touching earth that probably hadn't felt the gaze of sunlight in hundreds of years. At one point, Amy took a big handful of dirt and held it close to her face, took deep breaths of it. "It smells like a museum," she said, "like something from the past."

My father came over one afternoon and knelt over the hole, careful not to set his knee down in the torn-up earth. "Son, your mom asked me to tell you that if you are going to keep digging this . . . hole, then you're going to have to do something about all this dirt."

I asked him if we could just spread it out evenly through the backyard, maybe heighten the ground by a few inches, but he said no.

"You see, son, we have all this grass and plant life in the backyard and if you just throw a blanket of dirt over all that, you're going to kill it all. No, you're just going to have to figure out a way to get this stuff out of here."

We used Amy's truck to haul the dirt away. We did it at night, once the lights all went out in the houses of our subdivision. We loaded the dirt onto a plastic tarp in the bed of her truck and drove down to the lake. Amy would back the truck right up to the edge of the water and we would pull on the tarp until the dirt was gone. The surface of the water would bubble as the earth drifted down, worked itself in with the silt and debris at the bottom of the lake. By the fifth week there was a report in the paper that the water level had risen even though there had been no rain in twelve days. That's how much dirt we were hollowing out of the ground.

One night, Hunter woke up thrashing in his sleeping bag, rolling from side to side dangerously near the mouth of the hole. When we finally got him awake, he told us that he'd dug too far in his dream, had felt the earth give easily under his shovel and that fire had come out of the cracks, spilling around his feet.

"We can't keep digging down," he told us. "We'll find mole people or molten lava or some underground ocean."

"Or China," Amy offered. "We'll come up in China. That would be embarrassing."

Hunter nodded in agreement. "Nothing good down there," he said.

°°

So we went sideways.

We started expanding, tunneling farther and farther underneath our town. We dug random patterns that looped in on themselves and spread from one edge of the town to the other. We dug tunnels high enough to let us walk upright that would quickly turn into tiny pinpoints, so small we had to wedge ourselves through to keep going, the earth scattering in pieces as we moved. We never worried about cave-ins or getting lost. We were young and felt invincible. You never think about dying when you're twenty-two and drunk driving or bungee jumping or digging ill-designed tunnels underneath your parents' house. Under the surface, the air was cool and slightly damp and we felt like we were moving through a haze, a dream world that held no possibility for pain or disaster. And then we had a few near misses on some small cave-ins, and pain and possible death seemed slightly more possible. So we started building structures to reinforce the walls of the tunnels. After that, we just kept moving, up and down, left or right.

Eventually, we added rooms that served as the heart for all the tunnels, the source for all these paths to come and go from. We made them wide and high and eventually started sleeping in them at night, when we couldn't dig anymore. My mother gave us food weekly, dropped bags of groceries into the hole in the backyard, where one of us would go pick them up. "Here's your snacks honey," she would tell me as she dropped the groceries down the hole. I wore sunglasses to protect my eyes from the light that shined down on me. I was covered in dirt; it was under my fingernails and behind my ears. My mother was not pleased. "Honey, do you think that maybe it's all the marijuana that's making you do this?" I reached for another bag of groceries and shrugged. "I don't know," I told her. "I don't think so." I didn't know how to tell her that I was actually happy for the first time since college had ended. I had a purpose. I had to dig. I don't think she would have understood even if I had told her.

We found time capsules that had been forgotten and never dug up. Amy made up stories for each memento, giving new pasts to the objects we found before we sealed the capsules again. We always put them close to the surface, poking out of the ground slightly, where someone might notice the glint of sunlight reflecting off the silver canister.

There were a surprising number of jars filled with money. Old people must have buried them and then forgotten where they were. They were stuffed full of moldy tens and twenties, folded and wrapped in rubber bands, the jars sealed tight with paraffin wax. We found Styrofoam McDonald's containers and metal poles that had sunk into the ground and been forgotten. We found animal bones and human bones, and the still-decomposing body of Jasper Cooley, a drunk who had disappeared a few months ago. We couldn't find any signs of why he died and the clothes he was wearing were nice, even covered in dirt and bugs. Amy had found him, scraping her shovel against the rubber soles of his shoes until she finally realized what they were. Hunter and I worked carefully to fully remove him, careful of the decomposition that was taking place. Finally, we carried him in a sheet of plastic all the way back to one of the rooms. We propped him up against the wall until we could think of what to do about him. Hunter wanted to take him above-ground, leave him where someone could find him and give him a proper burial. "He's properly buried right now, Hunter," Amy said. "For all intents and purposes." But Hunter did not like this answer and so Amy and I had to dig a grave in the floor of the room, digging deeper into the ground. We had a ceremony and said a prayer and felt somehow better.

We ate sandwiches and listened to the faint noise of people and cars and machinery aboveground. We had portals all over town, tiny, obscured openings in the earth, which we could pop out of if we ever wanted to. But we never did; instead we spent all our time underground, digging more tunnels, coming out only in the middle of the night to dump the dirt in the lake. We were trying to hollow out a new world under the earth, to fill up the one above us.

Our shovels bit into the earth until they disintegrated, finally worn down to the wooden handle. We used the money from the sealed jars to buy new ones, pure titanium that my father got from the hardware store. He lowered them down to me one night, telling me, "These are the best they got. Good, dependable shovels." I took each one he handed down and bundled them together as well as I could. He also handed down boxes of batteries, and more flashlights, candles, and lanterns. "Mom and I aren't quite sure what you're doing down there," he whispered to me, stooped low over the hole. "We hope it's nothing we've done, but we just want you to be happy. So, if you have to be underground to be happy, that's fine with us." His hand came down through the hole and I shook it. Finally, we both walked away in the same direction, him on the surface of the earth and me below it. I imagined his footsteps above me as I moved.

At night, when our day of digging was over, we would gather in one of the main rooms and eat our dinner. We talked about our days, where we had dug, and what kind of soil we'd encountered. We loved to talk about dirt now. We all knew the wonderful feeling of digging into a new kind of soil. There was something transforming about watching the earth change as you dug and then passing through it, feeling yourself changed in the process. We were seeing the secrets of the earth revealed in tiny increments. It was better than drugs. Though we still did the drugs. There wasn't a whole lot to do at night under the earth.

We smoked pot that Amy's brother dropped through one of the holes on the surface. We did not tell him about the tunnels, though. We didn't want him and his high school friends using the tunnels as make-out spots, littering them with empty beer cans and used condoms. We just said it was our new drop spot, and he was too bored to care much beyond that. At nights, we rolled joints and made shadow puppets on the walls with a spotlight. Hunter could re-create *Apocalypse Now* in its entirety with only his two bare hands, twisting and flexing in the light, while Amy and I watched the shadows of his hands against the wall. He would make the bald head of Marlon Brando with his hands curved into a dome while he murmured, "The horror . . . the horror." We felt like cavemen, discovering all the various ways we could amuse ourselves. When we finally went to sleep, we dreamed of tunnels, endless, perfect structures that led us to some unknown place that we knew was heaven. Amy, the Gender Studies major, kept saying that there were Freudian theories based on these kinds of dreams but I really think that sometimes a tunnel is just a tunnel.

Hunter was tunneling one afternoon with Amy close behind him with her garden trowels, smoothing the passages. He hit something with his shovel, which he assumed to be rock. He traded off for the other shovel he had, the sharp, pointed one, and tried to work his way around. After an hour, he realized the rock spread out for at least ten feet on either side. "There's a boulder in the way," he told Amy, but kept chipping away. These kinds of things had become fun to us now.

Finally, he felt the rock give and saw light burst into the tunnel, filling up the passage. Hunter poked his head inside the hole and looked around the Corning family's basement. He'd broken through the cinder-block wall of their basement, which had been turned into a recreation room for the children. The Corning children stared back at him, the Foosball table no longer in action. "Sorry," he told them. "I must have the wrong house. I'm so sorry." He and Amy started backtracking, filling the tunnel back in and feeling terrible about the whole thing. That night, we all sat around in one of the main rooms and thought about how the Corning children were going to be punished tonight by their parents for destroying the wall in the basement. Actually, perhaps we didn't feel all that terrible about it. Perhaps we laughed for a long time. In all honesty, I am pretty sure that we laughed for a long time.

And then it was November and cold. We took all three of our sleeping bags and zipped them together to make one large bag to hold all of us. Covered in dirt, teeth chattering, we huddled against one another and waited for morning, or what we suspected was morning. The truth was that we had no idea for the most part. We dug until we were tired and then we slept. With both of their bodies covering my own, I felt the breath enter and leave their bodies, their hearts beating. And if there's any chance of being happier than that—filthy, cold, and almost imperceptible from the ground we slept on—I would like to know how.

But it got colder. The ground was more resistant to our shovels, and the metal spades wore down even faster. We ran out of money and had to make do with what was left. My parents were providing only the bare essentials now; they said it was hard to support three kids, especially when only one of them was their own. I understood, did not begrudge them this fact. We were finding the limits of what we could do and even though we acknowledged them, we had no idea what to do about it. We just kept digging.

Even though we still made new tunnels, we always seemed to find ourselves near the original hole by the end of the day. We would eat our dinner, crackers and bottles of water, and peek out to look at the stars. A few times, we climbed all the way to the top of the hole, looked over at my parents' house, warm and well lit, and then slowly crawled back into our tunnels. Our food was nearly gone. Our tools were broken. Our bodies were tired. We knew it was time to leave but it seemed difficult to say out loud. We scratched in the dirt with a stick, weighed the pros and the cons. Whoever wanted to leave could leave, no questions asked. In the morning, Hunter was gone, the sleeping bag smaller by one. Three days later, with no new tunnels dug, Amy kissed me on the cheek and wriggled out of the sleeping bag and then it was just me and the entire earth below the surface. It was a little lonely.

I tried to refill the tunnels but the work was much harder than hollowing them out. I had only one shovel left, nicked and dinged and inefficient. I finally gave up and crawled back to the main room and waited for something to happen. I lit one of the few candles left and tapped on the walls of the tunnel, *di-di-di-dah-dah-dah-di-di-di*. SOS.

A few nights later, I felt a hand on my shoulder and I pulled myself deeper into the sleeping bag, afraid of what was inside the tunnel with me. And then I heard my father speak. "Son," he said, "it's just me and your mom." I peered out of my sleeping bag and saw the bright light of a headlamp and my father's face beneath it. My mother was close behind him, holding a candle. "Your friends called us," he continued. "They wondered if you had left yet. I think they may be wanting to come back, feel like they've disappointed you." I shook my head, said that I didn't know if I was ready to leave. I couldn't imagine life above-ground, or, if I did, it seemed less tenable than what I had. "It's winter now," my father said. "It's getting cold. Less daylight." My mother then said, "It's time to come back up." They told me that they would let me live in the house with them for a while, until I could find my own place. My father had talked to a friend about getting me a job with his landscaping firm. They had contacted a psychiatrist whom I could talk to. They made it seem very plausible. I grabbed my shovel and then took a plastic shopping bag and filled it with dirt and then, one by one, we climbed out of the hole and walked back to the house.

I don't talk to Hunter or Amy anymore, though I heard that Hunter was in Alberta, spelunking around in Castleguard Cave on some grant from the North American Society. And Amy is getting her Ph.D. in geology and publishing some articles revolving around gender and mining. I'm still doing landscaping work, digging and planting and hauling. I ended up seeing the psychiatrist for a year. He said that I had been postponing my life, that hiding in the tunnels had been a way to avoid the responsibilities of the real world. And yes, that is true. I knew that the minute we started digging. But it was more than that. I don't know what it was, but I know it was more than that.

Sometimes, when work is over and I'm gathering up the

equipment and supplies, I place my hand flat against the ground and I feel the *thump, thump, thump* run through my body like Morse code. I listen for a long time to the sound of the earth and then I realize that it is just my heart, and the things it is saying are indecipherable. I dig my fingers into the freshly tilled ground, scoop up a handful of dirt, and feel happy again, happier than anything on earth, anything on top of the earth.

the shooting man

It took me damn near a week to convince Sue-Bee to come watch this guy shoot himself in the face. "Why would I wanna do something like that, Guster?" she asked me, which seemed like a dumb question because why does anyone want to do anything? It just seemed like fun, that's all.

I'd seen a sign for the show a couple weeks earlier, at the bowling alley where me and Hiram were rolling a few after we got off work at the noise factory. I was trying to save a 7–10 split when Hiram zipped a dime against my head and I turned around to face him. Down at the noise factory, you can't hear a thing for the nine hours you're there, even during breaks in the soundproof booth, so whenever Hiram needs me to correct a drill press or something, he flicks a coin at me. I don't know why he does it outside the factory.

"Guster, get a load of that poster over there. It's that guy, that Bullet guy Ellis was talking about."

We walked over to the bar, where this big colored poster was tacked up, glossy like magazine paper. It was for the Southeastern Oddities Revue, a traveling sideshow, and several of the performers were pictured, their faces stuck inside of yellow stars. There were three people in the outside stars that hovered near the edges of the poster, people called Magyar the Cigarette King, Jenny the Octopus Lady, and Lanny the Card Shark. They all seemed pretty nice, like something you'd waste a weeknight on, but it was the man in the middle of the poster, the man in the big star, that interested us. He was a handsome man, with a square jaw and blue eyes. He had a broad smile and one of those beards that only grows out of your chin and comes down in a point, like a V or something. He was holding a pearl-handled gun, with a curl of smoke lifting out of it. Above his star, in letters almost as big as the name of the sideshow company, it read: MAXIMILLIAN BULLET.

We'd heard a lot about him from Ellis, the foreman on our floor at the factory. He'd seen him several weeks earlier while visiting a cousin in Mobile. "Damndest thing, boys," he said when he came back to work that Monday "Damndest thing I ever saw."

This is what Ellis told us he saw in Mobile. This Bullet guy walked onto the stage, picked up a gun off of a little side table, placed it against his forehead, and pulled the trigger. "I saw things come out the back of that man's head I don't ever want to think about," Ellis told us, his eyes still a little glazed over.

Ellis said the guy was fine the next night because his cousin went to see it again in the next town over and this Bullet guy did it again. Hiram and me figured it was blanks in the gun and some special effects taped to the back of his head. Ellis disagreed when we mentioned it. "That's not what I saw," he told us. "That crazy fool blowed his brains out. Hand to God that's what he did." And no matter what we tried to say otherwise, Ellis wouldn't hear a word of it. He knew what he saw and so Hiram and me both decided we'd have to see it for ourselves, draw our own conclusions.

After work that day, I went home and told Sue-Bee all about the show, about Maximillian Bullet. I told her not to make any plans for that Friday, to wear something pretty. However, she was not happy with me, which was not entirely uncommon in the seven months we'd been living together. We were finding out that we both had strong feelings, and as hard as we tried to forget about them in the name our relationship, we sometimes cut into each other with the things we did. We spent a lot of time trying to remind ourselves that we were in love, and love demands sac- rifices. Even when you know the other is being a damned fool.

Sue-Bee did not want to see this show. She said it was sick to go watch someone do bad things to himself. I kept telling her that it wasn't real. I just wanted to see how real it was, how close he'd get to making me believe. And that seemed to me like a good answer, but she kept on scrubbing the dishes with that frown on her face, like she can't quite believe she sleeps in the same bed with me. Sue-Bee breaks my heart a lot, makes me realize I have no business being with someone as gorgeous and good-hearted as she is. She's got a way of making a man feel guilty for certain things he'd never feel bad about on his own, like watching someone shoot himself in the face.

⁘

I first met Sue-Bee at the dynamite demonstration. She'd orga- nized a group of people to come to the lake that weekend and protest against using dynamite to catch fish, a practice that had been going on for a few years now in the area and was supposedly damaging the ecosystem, at least this is what I learned later. I'd been driving by that afternoon to get a snow cone at the bait shop/snack bar. As I ate my cone on the park bench by the shop, I saw Sue-Bee, the determined way she held up her sign: BLOWING UP FISH IS WRONG! She stood in the middle of the group, and they all seemed focused on her, like they were waiting for her to do something. I tossed the snow cone in the trash and shuffled over to the protesters.

Just as I walked up to Sue-Bee, I saw Lester Mills stepping out of his boat. Lester and I had done our share of dynamite fishing late at night. He looked at the signs and then saw me standing there in the middle of the crowd. It looked like he was going to break out laughing right then. He waved to me, called my name, but I just looked away and pretended that I didn't know him from Adam. I just moved even closer to Sue-Bee. She smiled when she saw me, asked me if I was here for the demonstration, and I nodded yes. They handed me a sign that read, FISH DESERVE BETTER!, and I spent the entire day standing close beside her, looking away whenever one of my friends jumped into their boats.

After the demonstration, I took her to the Dairy Queen for ice cream and to talk about the demonstration. "If something makes you mad enough to think up slogans for a sign," she said, "then I say that is something you should be active in." I agreed with her, would have agreed with just about anything she said by that time. She'd been up north for college, and she was unbelievably smart, but not in a way that made you feel bad for not understanding her sometimes. I took her back to her parents' house after the Dairy Queen, and we made plans to see each other the next weekend. Later that night, I took my boat out in the twilight and gathered up the bloated fish rising to the surface, scooped up each one quickly even though I felt kind of bad about it.

°°

The next day at the noise factory, Hiram winged a penny against my ear, and when I turned around he held his arms up to question me about Sue-Bee and the sideshow. I shook my head no and went back to work. It's hard to concentrate in there sometimes, all the noise and whatnot. We put sound in things. My line puts the voice boxes in baby dolls, so all day long I hear the gurgled sounds of Chatty Cathy dolls. From seven to four, nothing but *waa-waa* and *Baby wants a bottle*. Hiram's got it worse, I suppose, putting *moo*s in those cow boxes that you turn upside down. Each line has a different set of noises but they all start to blend together. After a while, it fades into a humming that, even though you still hear it, doesn't really offend your ears.

°°

This shooting man was all anyone in town talked about. People had all kinds of ideas about him. He had a tube inserted into his head that allowed a bullet to pass through. He was an internal contortionist from Peru who could manipulate his brain to move out of the way of the bullets. He had escaped from a government testing facility that was inventing a race of people who could not be killed. They all seemed plausible at the time.

It was fun to try and figure out different ways this guy could shoot himself night after night and still live. I talked about it at the bowling alley, at the country ham bar after work, just about everywhere except at home, where Sue-Bee would not listen to a single explanation.

For the entire week leading up to the show, my days went like this: wake up, go to work, shake my head no to Hiram, go home, beg Sue-Bee, sleep. I pleaded with her, actually got down on my knees and tugged at the hem of her skirt like a little kid. "It's just not right, Guster," she would always reply, almost ashamed to have to say it. There were only two more days until the show and I didn't know how much more begging I could do. At night I dreamed about Maximillian Bullet, saw him put the gun in one ear and the bullet coming out the other.

◦◦

Hiram could not for the life of him understand what Sue-Bee was so hung up on.

"People shoot themselves in the face all the time," he said. "It's a grim reality."

"Yeah, but she says that doesn't mean we should watch them do it."

"Well, hell, she watches them nature shows on Discovery, watches big huge tigers rip poor little zebras all to hell and she don't bat so much as an eyelash. What do you call that?"

And I didn't know what to call that, but I knew it wasn't the same thing, that I was asking Sue-Bee to watch something she thought was wrong. I was beginning to understand that these were the things you denied yourself in the name of love, these wonderful happenings of an unfavorable nature. I thought about Sue-Bee and her kindness, her innocent ways of reducing the world to basic truths. I thought about the shooting man and the unspeakable things that could happen. I knew I would regret it, but I also knew what had to be done. And Hiram could whisper words under his breath all he wanted: *Soft. Tied down. Whipped. In love.*

So, that night when I came home, I didn't mention the shooting man, didn't beg or pout. She was reading a book in bed when I finally got back from the Bowl-go-Round and her hair was loose around her face, thin gold strands of hair that hung down like branches of a weeping willow. I stripped out of my coveralls, hung them up in the closet, and crawled into bed beside her. Sue-Bee's eyes are beautiful, even behind her reading glasses, big and deep and blue. I watched her read, the silent way her lips formed the printed words. I thought maybe she was talking to me, whispering things I couldn't quite hear, and she was beautiful. I kissed her, brushed her hair off her face, and rolled over to sleep. It's hard for me to relax most nights. Hours after the noise factory, I can still hear humming, and it takes a long time for sleep to overcome the sounds. As I squeezed my eyes tight, waited to wake up tomorrow, I heard Sue-Bee say something.

"You really want to see this fool don't you?"

I rolled over, rested my head in her lap. I told her that I wanted to see Maximillian Bullet more than just about anything else in the world.

"Then I suppose I'll go. I just don't want you to miss this and spend the rest of our time together thinking you'd been cheated out of something important. I don't want any responsibility for things you may have seen."

I kissed Sue-Bee fast on the mouth and wrapped her up in my arms, pushed the book to the floor. We curled up like two snakes wrapping themselves tight around the other, tighter and tighter until it seemed like there was only one of us in bed. Just before I drifted off, she asked me, "It's not real, right? It's just a show?" And I was finally losing the noises in my head, but before I dropped out of being awake I whispered to her, "Probably not."

The next morning at the noise factory, the day of the sideshow, I waited for a nickel or penny to smack against my ear. When it finally did, I looked behind me and saw Hiram. I made a gun with one of my hands and pressed it against my head, laughed, and fired. Hiram, surprised at Sue-Bee's allowance, laughed and did the gun thing with his hand too. And all through work, we sneaked glances at each other, placing our gun hands inside our mouths, against our temples, giggling like little kids.

⁖

Sue-Bee and me met Hiram and his girl outside the civic center where the show was being held. Hiram's girl, Miggy, was one of the rain machine workers at the factory. She seemed bored with the impending show, but the rest of us were wired, even Sue-Bee, who seemed excited despite herself. We paid for our tickets and found some good seats right in the middle of the bleachers. Sue-Bee kept squeezing my hand, tighter each time as we listened to the rising murmurs of the audience around us.

Magyar the Cigarette King came out first and pulled lit cigarettes out of his mouth and ears and nose. He smoked eighty-seven cigarettes at the same time, his mouth stretched around and his head obscured by a dense cloud of smoke. Miggy leaned back on the bleachers. "Nothing I couldn't do," she said. When he was done, Jenny the Octopus Lady juggled red rubber balls with her seemingly real four arms. She played Beethoven's 5th on two separate pianos at the same time, but all of us were so ready for Maximillian that people started growing impatient. By the time Lanny the Card Shark got onstage, the audience was yelling out for the star to appear. Lanny hurried through his tricks, spraying decks of cards around him like he was stuck in a tornado, and then ran offstage.

A stagehand ran out to the floor and set up a small card table, cluttered only by a pearl-handled revolver and a small white sign that read, FIVE MINUTES UNTIL MAXIMILLIAN! The exclamation point on the sign was made out of a gold bullet.

The lights in the gym died down, save for a spotlight pointed toward the revolver. We waited, each of us holding our breath until none of us thought we could stand one more second, that we would pass out if we didn't see him.

A voice called out over the loudspeakers, "Ladies and gentlemen, we warn you that what you are about to see will shock and amaze you. Direct from New York City, we offer for your enjoyment, the singular sensation of weapons acrobatics, the one and only Maximillian Bullet." The crowd filled the gym with applause, with whistles and cheers, and even Sue-Bee managed a few polite claps. In the center of the floor, we saw a figure appear, feet shuffling across the glossy hardwood. He wore a red cape that extended to his feet, made it almost seem as if he were floating, a black top hat, and a bow tie. His face was haggard, worn away with hunger and hard times. He looked older than he had appeared on the poster, a thick scruff replacing his v-shaped beard. In fact, Hiram whispered across Miggy at me, "That sure as hell don't look like the Maximillian from the poster."

Maximillian did not speak. He held the pistol limp in his right hand and walked closer to the crowd, the lights following him, almost touching the first row. His eyes darted quickly across the gym, but he still remained silent. Sue-Bee's hands were tight on my arm, her head pushed hard against my shoulder. I kept staring at the man, watching the way he stared back at us. He was looking up into the crowd, almost directly at me, and I nearly said something as he pressed the barrel of the gun into the space between his eyes. I felt something like a tiny yelp rush out of me, but I kept silent, stayed focused, and watched him shoot himself in the face.

Later, in the parking lot, Hiram said that he had seen the exiting bullet. When I saw the front of his face open up, flaps of skin and bone just peel away and hang in the air, I watched the way everything seemed to hold for that split second, just freeze like time had been so shocked that it couldn't quite remember to keep going. Sue-Bee pulled herself into me, wrapped her arms around my neck, and murmured, "It's just not right, Guster." I heard Hiram utter, "Be damned," then he fell silent again. I could still hear the cracking sound of the bullet leaving the gun, that sharp explosion like winter trees snapping in half.

Maximillian's feet lifted off the ground, as if he were being taken away from us, off to somewhere better, and then he fell backward, arms splayed and legs bent at funny angles. From where we sat, we could just make out the sight of blood dripping from his forehead like the expanding points of a star. Suddenly, the stagehand scurried across the floor with a wheelbarrow and scooped Maximillian into it. He then wheeled the body out of the gym, out of sight as we all sat there, dumb and unblinking and wondering what the hell we'd just seen. The loudspeaker voice exclaimed, "Thank you for attending, ladies and gentlemen. We would appreciate one more round of applause for the magnificent Maximillian Bullet. He will be performing in three days in Millersville, so please come watch this amazing man stare death in the face once again."

Some people clapped, but most just stood and filed out of the gym, too shocked to think straight. The gun was lying there on the floor, and I focused on it as I led Sue-Bee down the bleachers. When we got to the parking lot, there wasn't much to say. Hiram kept whispering, "Be damned." Finally, he told us that he and Miggy were going to go over to the country ham bar to drink until they were too drunk to dream about any of this. I helped Sue-Bee into the car and pulled out onto the road, the echo of the shot still clear in my head.

"I want you to take me to my parents' house," she said as we followed the other cars out of the parking lot and onto the highway. I damn near veered into oncoming traffic when I heard her.

"Why would you want me to do something like that?"

"Because I'm sad and it's your fault. I'm not going to share the same house with someone who made me watch that."

Her face was blotched red in patterns, and I thought it could make a picture if I looked hard enough, like those inkblot tests shrinks give you. Her eyes were thick with tears, almost wavy. I tried to slide my arm around her, pull her closer to the driver's seat, but she jerked away and focused on the road.

"It's just something you see," I told her. "It don't mean nothing."

"Just take me to my parents' house, Guster."

I pressed down hard on the accelerator, mumbled obscenities. I pulled up in front of the house, a nice two-story house in the good subdivision, but I refused to pull into the driveway. I wanted her to walk a little, I guess. When she stepped out of the car, I asked her when she thought she might come back. She leaned into the car and said she didn't know. So we just let it hang like that.

Just before she shut the door, I called out after her, "It's just a show, Sue-Bee, ain't a thing real about it." She either didn't hear me or didn't care to, because she ran up to the house and disappeared inside. I sat there for a little while, engine idling. I watched for shadows of movement behind the curtains in her old room. When I saw a figure moving slowly, head hung down,

I squealed my tires like the sound of pigs drowning and burned a black rubber path out of the subdivision, left a map for her to remember her way back to me.

I swung my car back down the road that led to the civic center, not really knowing what I reckoned to do, if anything. When I pulled into the parking lot, it was near empty; no one was milling around. I pushed open the door to the center and walked down the hallway, checking each door as I walked past. Inside the gym, I crept over to where Maximillian had done the shooting. There were smears of what looked like blood on the floor. I leaned down and dipped my fingers in it, felt the warmth of it, how it was already turning solid and gummy. The gun was still there and I kicked it, watched it spin across the hardwood floor and skitter under the bleachers. I could still hear it slowly spinning as I walked into the locker room, pressed my ear against the door, and slowly pushed it open. Inside, there were four men sitting around, smoking cigarettes and throwing cards down on the table. I cleared my throat, watched them slowly raise up to meet me.

"What do you reckon you're doing in here, mister?"

I fumbled around in my pockets and produced the ticket stub from the show.

"Wondering if I could maybe get that shooting man to sign this stub for my girl. Maybe make her feel a little better if she knew he was okay."

"Max has left already. You tell her to come see him in Millersville. She'll see he's absolutely okay, does this thing all the time."

In the corner of the room, I saw something wrapped up in plastic, propped up in the corner and slowly scraping across the wall as it fell to the ground.

"Look, you have to leave now. Come to Millersville, we'll make sure you meet him then."

I pointed at the figure as I began to back away.

"He sure don't look much like the man on the poster."

One of the men stood up out of the chair and pulled me back into the room.

"Nothing looks much like you 'spect it will, do it?"

◦◦
◦◦

The men explained it to me as best they could, as best anyone could explain something like that. They told me I had two choices. They could just kill me right then and dump the body in a hole and fill it with concrete. Or I could join up, take on the part. It was an easy decision.

I spend a lot of time now on one of the tour buses, filled with all the other Maximillian Bullets. There are twenty-six of us at the moment. They are quiet, nervous men, all of them. They have stubble and deep eyes that you cannot stare at for too long or you will figure out things you don't want to know. It's a little surprising, how bad things must be for so many people to be willing to trade up for a few weeks of quiet. It is scary to know that there are things in our lives where shooting yourself in the face is preferable.

They take good care of us before we go. We get all our meals paid for, a new set of clothes, lots of free time. We also get free tickets to every show, but none of the other Maxes use them. I do though, have seen a lot of men send bullets through their heads since I joined up. It doesn't do much to me now. I can hardly hear the gunshot anymore. I just sit up there in the crowd with my free popcorn and soda and I watch real close. I look for any angle, the way they place the gun to their foreheads. I wonder what's going through their minds, if they're thinking about what they've left behind. I watch real close.

I've got an idea now. I am almost certain I can do it, can take the bullet. It's getting closer to my show time. There are only two or three guys before me now. I don't do much anymore besides watch the shows. I sit on the bus and stare out the window, thinking about Sue-Bee. I think about her eyes, the way they held happy and sad. I want to go back to her.

I think I can do it. I will walk out on the stage. I will pick up the gun, press it tight against my head, and pull the trigger. I will fall awkwardly, feel a ripping in the back of my head. I will lie there on the ground for maybe two or three minutes. And then I will stand up, wave my arms in the air for the crowd, and they will cheer like no one has ever cheered for Maximillian Bullet. They will throw pennies and dimes onto the gym floor and I will walk out of the building in a shower of coins, right past the owners of the show. And I will keep walking. I will find my way back to Sue-Bee and knock on her door. When she answers, I will show her the hole and then pull her close to me. I will show her I'm okay, that I made it. I'll show her it ain't so bad.

the choir director affair
(the baby's teeth)

this is the baby, and yes, those are teeth. They are not important. Don't think about them. Nothing special, this baby with teeth. Usually it is only a snaggletooth, a single, perfectly formed tooth in the tiny mouth, unlike the full set on this baby. Still, it has happened before, is happening now, will happen again, Jesus Christ, get over it. It is nothing to get upset about. They are only teeth. So forget we even mentioned it because it doesn't matter: the baby, the teeth, the pacifiers gnawed until they are unrecognizable.

The story isn't about the baby anyway, but the father of the baby. He is having an affair with the choir director of the girls' chorus at the private school where he teaches biology. There is guilt and lust and deceit and the things that stories are made of, the condition of our collective lives laid bare. And yet, this baby.

When you are invited to visit the parents just a few weeks after the birth, you walk into the newly decorated, mobiled, yellow-hued room and you coo and baby talk over this new thing, this well-made construction of genes. And then the baby flashes those teeth and you . . . well, you scream.

The father, who is sleeping with a beautiful, red-haired woman who sings like a bird, calmly informs you about the teeth, repeating what the doctors said, the pamphlets the hospital had to order from a medical oddities supplier. The wife, who does not know about the affair but knows her husband has things he keeps from her, starts to tear up, until she has to excuse herself for a moment. You feel like a real son of a bitch but why wouldn't someone have mentioned this beforehand? A small warning: this baby will smile and it will startle you.

However, the parents are preoccupied. For the father: a woman ten years younger than him, digging her fingernails into his back as he presses her onto a desk in the band room. For the mother: bruises on her nipples from breastfeeding, tiny bite marks that were once made by her husband but no longer. These are not earth-shattering things but they can, if necessary, keep you from examining other aspects of your life.

Later that night, while the mother flosses the baby and prepares it for sleep, you sit in the kitchen and drink beer while the husband tells you about the choir director and how she hits impossibly high notes when she climaxes. He says he is racked with guilt, especially with a new baby to think about, but you can tell he is pleased with himself. A woman sings because of him and no amount of hand-wringing can hide that. He tells you that she has a split uvula and that it drives him crazy just thinking about it when she goes down on him. Now you are a little disgusted, the easy, animal ways that he can get off on the genetic peculiarities of others. With his baby lying in bed upstairs with all those teeth.

You try to listen to the rest, the times and places and ways. You think you hear the father say that he is falling in love with this woman, but you cannot concentrate. You want to. You know this is the thing that matters, the thing that will affect all their lives in myriad ways, but you cannot do it.

You excuse yourself, blame the beer, and seek the bathroom. Upstairs, down the hall, and into the room, quiet save for the hiss of a humidifier. The baby is still awake, eyes wide open. You smile a little nervously, not wanting to cause alarm. And the baby, goddamn, smiles right back. Big and wide.

If, in less than a year, this baby were to sprout its teeth naturally, you would think nothing of it. In fact, you'd be a little annoyed, the constant crying, the blue plastic toy pulled from the freezer and jammed into the mouth. Now, however, in the dim light of the baby's room, they are inexhaustibly fascinating. Calcified, enameled, not yet cavitied. They really are the color of a pearl. You have heard that cliché of toothpaste commercials that show the tube, the brush, the tiny sparkle that shines off the front tooth, but now you understand the phrase. You think this baby's teeth could be used as a necklace, something beautiful and perfect.

Now your hand is moving toward the baby, slowly, index finger extended, as if pointing to a place on a map. You touch the smoothness of one of the teeth, the rounded edge on the bottom. The baby's eyes stay open, calm, but you do not see them, only the teeth. And then the teeth closing around your finger, quickly. Your finger is still there, in the mouth, and now there is skin to be broken, cries to be muffled, shots to be considered.

This was not supposed to happen. You were supposed to stay downstairs with the father and listen to him go on and on about this singing adulteress. Instead, you are wrapping your finger in tissues, bounding quickly down the stairs, wondering aloud where the time went, hugging the father in order to avoid a handshake and reveal the offending finger, and running to your car before you sit there in silence. You are not listening to the father and his newfound desire to perhaps leave his wife and child and run off to Europe with this choir director to visit old opera houses. You are not there to witness this total lack of judgment and decency and advise yea or nay.

As of this moment, you in the car, staring at those teeth impressions on your finger, you think the father's dalliance will not last much longer and will hopefully cause only a small amount of unhappiness, which is not true, of course. Why would we be telling this story if that were the case? But none of this matters to you now as you speed through the night, the radio playing in your car, the windows down, your finger in your own mouth, your tongue finding the impressions left by teeth much smaller than your own.

The gravity of the situation, the mother and father and choir director, becomes abundantly clear to you not long after that night. You are the friend of the father and so now you have become something more than that: an alibi. You are doing more with the father than you ever have before, though you actually just sit at home in your underwear and read orthodontia journals. Still, in theory, in the mind of the mother, you are hitting balls at the driving range together, going to see the Double A baseball team, sitting in on lectures at the Museum of Natural

History about the eating habits of tree frogs. You are doing so much together, though actually apart, that the mother, who is now beginning to suspect something, begins to believe that perhaps it is you with whom the father is having an affair.

The father will tell you this over coffee one night, the first time you've actually seen him in weeks. He will relate the late-night accusation from the mother, the baby held in her arms like a threat, chewing on a squeaky dog toy in the shape of a fire hydrant. The father will laugh, the same way he is laughing right now as he tells you this, and calm his wife, take the baby out of her arms, and bounce it softly against his chest. She will cry, apologize, and they will make love for the first time since the baby was born, soft and cautious at first. Finally, their own fears and questions will come out and they will bang the bed frame against the wall, the springs squeaking in a rhythm that matches the baby monitor's transmission of the dog toy in the mouth of the baby. And even after they are finished, when they separate and sleep facing opposite directions, there will be the sound of the baby chewing, squeaking, telling them things they either don't want to think about or already know.

You receive a photo Christmas card from the family and what you should notice is the formal distance between the mother and the father, the grim look of finality on their faces. You don't notice this at all because of that damn baby, wearing a Santa hat and grinning. You can barely make it out, but you get out a magnifying glass and yes, those are the teeth. You put the photo in a frame and it sits beside your bed. At night, after you talk to the husband and agree on his next alibi, you hold the picture close to your face. You squint your eyes and if you try hard enough, you pretend that the parents aren't there at all, their malaise and distrust brushed right off the photo. Instead it is the baby, that hat, those teeth, and, of course, you holding the baby, arms outstretched as if to say, "Look at this, how perfect, how wonderful." And this, again, tells us just what you are getting out of this story, the wrong things.

Why do you spend so much of your time in your underwear? We just find it curious. Every time we bring the story to your house . . . never mind, no matter. In any case, you are in your underwear when the father knocks on your door, holding the baby like a salesman about to tell you why you simply must have this baby, cannot say no to this remarkable invention. And you, sans pants, look as if you would pay any amount, if only you could find that wallet.

There has been a complication. The reading by a famous novelist who has written a book about birds and love and architecture that you are going to hear tonight with the father has been compromised. It was already compromised by the fact that the father and the choir director were instead going to a restaurant three towns over and then having sex in a motel and looking at a travel book about Austria. And you were going to do . . . whatever it was you were going to do in your own house with no pants. Now though, there are further problems.

The wife is not feeling well. When she asked the father if he could cancel his plans to see the novelist read, he said he really couldn't. You are a lover of the arts and plans had been made and you are supposedly very high-strung about keeping one's appointments. So the wife asked him to bring the baby. Serious readings about birds and love and architecture are no place for babies but the wife was too busy throwing up to listen to anything else. So this explains the house call, the baby, the dim shadow of a woman in the car, waiting patiently.

What you should now grasp is that the mother knows about

the affair. She knows even who the person is, the choir director. This knowledge has made her ill, sick in mysterious ways to the husband, who is so wrapped up in his fantasies about himself and the choir director that he has no idea that he has been discovered. This was bound to happen though, the way in which a marriage so easily becomes something less than that, two people bound by things they can't quite remember.

You take the baby in your arms, carry it over the threshold into your home with a baby bag slung over your shoulder, as if the two of you are going on a trip from which you may never want to return.

You set the baby on the coffee table and this is the only thing either of you can think to do for some time. You smile, make baby faces. The baby smiles back, politely. You make hand gestures to say my house is your house, and the baby keeps smiling and you realize this is really all you want. You decide it's best to put on pants, wonder if the father even noticed your lack of them.

Inside the plaid baby bag filled with diapers and formula and wipes is the baby's dinner. No strained peas for this baby, no Dutch apples. Two Big Macs. *Cut them into bite-sized pieces.* That is what the father told you, which you thought a strange request at the time. You take one of the Big Macs out of its box, saving the other for yourself, and the baby's wriggling hands reach out toward the hamburger. You tear off a piece and hold it toward the baby, who opens its mouth, revealing the teeth. You drop the food in quickly, now wary of the power and sharpness of those teeth. There is no hesitation for the baby. It has done this before. You work quickly, tearing the hamburger apart, feeding it to those teeth that mash and gnash it into something that resembles normal baby food. You wipe away the special sauce from the baby's mouth. This makes the baby smile, which makes you smile, and with dinner over, there is nothing to do but stare, enjoy each other's company.

You make a little bed out of blankets and pillows but it seems insubstantial. You hold the baby instead and rock it to sleep, aided by the heaviness of the Big Mac being digested. The baby pulls itself into you, softly kicks its feet as it drifts away. You begin to think that perhaps you actually love this baby, not just the teeth inside of it. You lean back against the sofa and fall asleep. In your arms, the baby silently grinds its soft teeth together, not quite asleep, not quite awake.

Then there is the knock on the door, the transaction of baby between you and the father. It is silent, without thanks or welcome. The father would rather not take it. You would rather keep it. So it goes. There are other things to consider: the mother, laws of nature, financial obligations, keeping up appearances. Nonetheless, this is the long and the short of it, the essential fact. Someone wants something the other does not and unhappiness ensues. It is also the essential fact of the more important thing, the father and the affair and his family. So it goes.

In the coming months, there will be many things. Fights, accusations, declarations of love and hate. It is heartbreaking, but you only want to know of the baby, where it is, what it is doing, is it smiling. We have grown tired. The story is hard to tell. The evaporation of love makes us think of our own lives. We have tried to make you see this, but always the baby. So here.

Here is the baby in its room, bobbing up and down in a bouncy chair, forgotten for the moment by his parents, who are in the kitchen. They are arguing, but quietly, under the surface. Too much sugar in one's coffee, newspaper folded and refolded in the face of questions, mentions of after-school activities.

In its room, however, the baby forces its hands into its mouth, sharp fingernails jabbing and scraping its gums with each bounce. Nothing to occupy its time, the unceasing rhythm of the chair keeping it from sleep, the baby chews on its fingernails, gnawing until its teeth tear into the quick. Thin crescents of blood wax and wane across the tips of its fingers.

When the parents, sick of their proximity to each other without a buffer, arrive at the doorway of the baby's room, they find that they cannot cross the threshold. It takes all their power to keep from making a single sound. There, so close to them they cannot look away, is the baby, fingers speckled with tiny drops of blood, lips red and wet, smiling.

There is the inevitable. The separation, the divorce, the trip to Vienna. The baby with teeth stays with the mother, who stays in her house and rarely leaves. The father sends you a postcard of the Wiener Staatsoper, an opera house so beautiful you begin to think the father left his old life behind not for the choir director but for this building. The back of the postcard reads simply: "Having a wonderful time."

The father will soon not be having a wonderful time. The choir director will leave him after they return to the States. His job at the school is rescinded for his indiscretions. His hair begins to fall out. The mother will not allow him to visit the baby. He calls you one night and asks if you will check on them, that he is worried about the mother and the baby. Of course he is worried, but what he is truly worried about is if they will take him back.

You go, knock, say hello, sit down for coffee. The mother is telling you that she does not blame you for any of this. This should make you happy but you are not listening. You are watching the baby in its high chair in the kitchen. From the sofa, you can just barely see the baby. It is chewing something—bubble gum you realize. And are those bubbles? You cannot be sure. Perhaps. The mother is still talking. Then she is not. Then she is kissing you. It is time to leave. You call the father and tell him the baby is fine.

Years and years later, you will see the baby again, though it is no longer a baby. The baby is a teenager now, sullen, acned, unaccustomed to its body. The baby works at the grocery store, swiping your items and taking your money. The baby with teeth no longer smiles, no matter how hard you try. And even if the baby were to smile, just a tiny bit, there would be nothing wondrous about it. There would be teeth, the same as anyone else. Perhaps even braces. The things you thought so amazing about this baby are no longer there, and this makes you inescapably sad.

And as you look one more time at this baby you once thought the world of, perhaps we have shown you the thing we intended all along. You hand a bag of carrots to the former baby with teeth. Your hands touch briefly. There is nothing, only the transaction of an item. Nothing more. You hand over the rest of the items from your cart and as the old baby reaches over to scan each offering, you begin to understand. Don't you see? The things we once loved do not change, only our belief in them.

Now, right now, you stare at the baby there in the checkout line, and then it is over. You are left with the only things that any of us have in the end. The things we keep inside of ourselves, that grow out of us, that tell us who we are.

go, fight, win

She was a cheerleader, but she was beginning to realize that she had made a mistake. Simply put, Penny didn't care if the football team ever won a game, and the fact that other people did care, and relied on her to make them care even more, made her feel like a liar. During pep rallies, she couldn't remember the words to all of the cheers, and from time to time she would randomly shout one of three words, *go* or *fight* or *win*. It was amazing to her how often she was correct.

The only thing she was good at, the reason she suspected that she had made the team at all, were her handsprings, perfect and unending. She could flip the length of the gymnasium floor, though this made her nervous, the sudden, irrational fear in mid-tumble that she wasn't wearing her undershorts. From the minute she ran onto the hardwood floor until she was back in the locker room, she felt like she was holding her breath, praying that no one would notice her. Still, there were moments when she stared into the bleachers filled with her classmates that she was glad she wasn't sitting with them, was at least at a slight distance from everyone else. If she could just get free of the other cheerleaders as well.

°°
°°

It was her mother who had forced her to try out for the squad. "You're pretty, Pen, real pretty, but you're new," her mother told her once they'd moved to Coalfield that summer, after her parents' divorce. "You're the kind of pretty that would benefit from being a cheerleader, you know?" Penny knew what her mom really wanted to say was that Penny was weird, too quiet, and no one was going to give her a chance unless she had something else going for her.

That first night in their new place, a duplex far away from the main part of town, Penny and her mother sat on the floor in the living room, surrounded by unopened boxes. While they ate their dinner, oranges and cheese sandwiches, her mother made a list of reasons that Penny should try out for the cheerleading squad. Each time she started to write something, Penny's mother would look up from the list and stare at her for about fifteen seconds before she started writing again.

For starters, Penny was pretty, with blond hair that was shiny and strong, though sometimes too frizzy. She had bright green eyes and just a light splash of freckles. Penny was athletic too; five years of gymnastics had given her good muscle tone. She was new but that could work to her advantage, as long as she didn't seem too stuck-up. She needed friends, and what better way to make new friends than to join up with the most popular girls at Coalfield High School? "Say you'll do it," her mother said, "just say you'll give it a shot." Penny read the list. It embarrassed her, the intense way that her mother treated her now, as if Penny were always dangerously close to making a fool of herself if she didn't focus. Penny crumpled up the paper and said, "I'll try." And though she did not say this to her mother, suspecting that she already knew, Penny did not want any part of this.

⁘

And now she was a cheerleader, three weeks into the football season and basketball waiting in the spring. She hadn't made any new friends and the one thing she'd always depended on, the ability to disappear, was gone. On game days, she had to wear her cheerleading uniform at school, and she constantly pulled at the skirt, which seemed at least two inches too short.

And even on the other days, she had to sit with the rest of the cheerleaders at their special table near the soda machines in the cafeteria, where Penny chewed each bite slowly just to avoid having to talk. Not that the other girls, who had known each other since grade school and lived in subdivisions that were nowhere near Penny's house, asked her many questions. It wasn't that they were mean; Penny knew this. They were simply uneasy around her, how little she gave them to work with. One time, when Michelle Rainey made a joke that Penny didn't understand, she laughed along with the other girls until Michelle looked puzzled and asked Penny, "How do you know about that?" Penny shook her head and looked down at her tray, which was nearly empty. She grabbed a celery stick and took small bites until Michelle shrugged her shoulders and kept talking.

She felt angry with her mother but even more with herself.

She had agreed to try because she had hoped, in her most secret moments, that things would work, that she would feel calm and happy and completely different from the person that she was. But nothing changed and when she turned backflips at the pep rallies, she mumbled curse words with each ragged exhalation of breath.

∷

After practice, Penny rode home with the Bakers, a black couple who worked as janitors at the school and lived in the other half of the duplex that Penny and her mother shared. Her mother worked until 10:30 each night at the hospital, sometimes even later. Since she was new, her mother worked the shifts that other nurses didn't want, sixty hours a week, and so Penny and her mother were on different schedules, always walking into the duplex when the other was gone. It was slightly embarrassing, the other girls climbing into cars while she stayed behind, waiting for the Bakers to finish up their cleaning. At the start of the year, some of the girls had offered her a ride home, but she always declined; the thought of making conversation set off something sharp and painful in her stomach. Soon they stopped asking, which suited Penny just fine.

On the car ride home, windows down while the Bakers smoked and gospel music crackled from the speakers on the right side of the car, Penny rested her head against the back seat and closed her eyes. She liked the smell of the car, cleaning supplies and menthol cigarettes, and she appreciated the fact that neither of the Bakers thought anything of the fact that Penny hardly talked. They made enough conversation between the two of them, discussing notes they had found in the garbage cans and gossip about the teachers. When they pulled up to the duplex, Mrs. Baker nudged Penny and motioned to the house across the street.

"You know that boy?" she asked Penny.

Sitting on the steps of the house directly across from Penny, a boy about ten or eleven years old, though he was tall and gangly enough to look adolescent, flicked matches into a plastic cup, striking them on the box and then tossing them with a quick flick of his wrist. When he noticed that Penny was looking at him, he stopped, holding one of the matches between his thumb and index finger, and stared back at her. He had fine blond hair that was curly enough to make it look messy, and his face was strangely proportioned, small eyes and nose and almost delicate ears, which gave way to chubby cheeks and a mouth filled with too many teeth and the mere suggestion of a chin. His shirt was ripped at the neck and he was barefoot, his toes stained red with clay. Penny thought he looked like a cartoon character.

"I don't know him," she said.

"That boy's been watching you from that house every day this week," said Mrs. Baker, laughing a little. "And you say you don't know a thing about him?"

Penny shook her head. The match in the boy's hand was still burning, nearly touching his fingers now.

"Well, he's watching you," she continued. "He's slightly touched, I think. Don't go to school, just stays at home all day. I remember last year, maybe the year before last, he made some kind of flying machine, like a backpack with wings, and he jumped off the roof and fell almost two stories. A wonder he didn't break his neck. I didn't see it, but Jeffrey saw it, didn't you?"

The flame disappeared from the boy's hand and he put his fingers in his mouth. It looked like he was smiling.

Mr. Baker stubbed out his cigarette in the ashtray and exhaled, still not answering. He looked like he was remembering the event and trying to decide if it had really happened. "Glided for about six or seven feet and then spun sideways and slammed back into the side of that house and landed flat on his damn back. He just jumped up, looked around, and ran inside. One hell of an odd thing to witness. He give you trouble, Penny, you tell me and I'll run him off."

"I don't know him," Penny said. "I've never seen him."

"Best if it stays that way," Mrs. Baker said.

∷

Inside the house, Penny finished her homework, though she couldn't help sneaking to the window and peering through the blinds. The boy was gone now, but still she checked. When she had finished all of her lessons for the next day, she went to her closet and reached for a box on the top shelf. It was a model for a 1965 Pontiac GTO, a plastic 1/25th replica. She took the box down and set it on the floor of her room. Then she spread a piece of wax paper over her desk and opened the drawer and pulled out a tiny brush and a tube of model glue. After she opened the box, she set out each piece and then took the instructions over to the bed and lay down and stared at every panel until she was sure she knew what she was doing. And for the rest of the night, she carefully unsnapped each piece from the frame and set it in place, watching with a silent happiness the way the car came together, seemed to appear from nothing but the movement of her hands.

She had been making models for a few years now, her favorite thing. She didn't actually care about the cars, only the task of creating them. Once she was finished, she kept the model car on her desk for a few weeks, until her memory of making it began to fade. Then she would toss the car in the garbage and start another one. They were expensive, fifteen dollars apiece, sometimes more, and she had to budget carefully. Her father sent her twenty dollars a week and she still had some money from babysitting when she lived back in Kingston. But she had clothes to buy and cheerleading dues to consider. She set aside a little money each week and, when she had enough, she rode her bike over to the hobby shop in the Town Square and bought whatever looked interesting, a 1932 Ford Phaeton or a 1971 Plymouth Duster. She had made a few airplanes and a figure model of Dr. McCoy from *Star Trek* but they weren't as interesting to her as the model cars. She liked the clean lines of the automobiles, the shiny chrome of the hubcaps. The man who ran the hobby shop had told her one of the first times she came to the shop, "I got a real-life 1962 Chevy Impala out back if you want to see it." She stammered for a few seconds and said that she didn't like real-life cars that much. "Well, models are nice," he told her, "but ain't never as good as the real thing." She reached for her model and walked out of the store. The next time, she bought a model car at Wal-Mart, but it was flimsy and not nearly as difficult to build. After a while, she went back to the hobby shop and tried not to make eye contact with the man in the store.

∞

She had finished nearly the entire base of the car when her mother finally came home. Penny met her in the kitchen and helped her set the table for dinner. It was nearly 11:30, and Penny hadn't eaten since lunch, but she didn't feel hungry. While they ate soup and salad from the hospital cafeteria, her mother told her about a man who'd gotten drunk and let people punch him in the stomach over and over. It wasn't until the next day that he noticed he had blood in his urine and he could taste something metallic in his mouth. "Ruptured something," she told Penny, "and he seemed so shocked, too, that was the weird thing. It took him forever to remember why he might have all this blood in his pee." Penny looked down at her minestrone soup and made a face, then pushed it away. They sat in silence for the rest of the meal.

Once they'd washed the dishes, Penny kissed her mother and went back to her room. Before she shut the door, she heard her mother call out.

"Sometimes, right when I pull up in the driveway, I think that you might be gone. I worry that you'll be out partying with all those girls, doing drugs or some other terrible thing. And then I open the door and you're always here."

Penny walked into the hallway and looked at her mother. She still had her nurse uniform on, and her hair was spilling out from underneath her hat. She had circles under her eyes, very faint but noticeable against her pale skin, but Penny thought that she still looked pretty. It seemed so strange when she thought about it, that now it was only she and her mother in this place, far from anyone they knew.

"I'm gonna be here, Mom," Penny said.

"I know you will, honey," she answered. "I know that."

Penny hugged her mother and had started back toward her room when her mom spoke again.

"But if you weren't here one time, I'd understand. I'd know that sometimes a girl has to get out there with her friends and have a little fun. You'd just have to tell me and then I'd know and it would be fine."

Penny didn't say anything, merely shut her door and then

stood over the unfinished model car as she inhaled the sharp scent of glue until she felt tired enough to go to sleep.

∷

The next afternoon, in the back of the Bakers' car, Penny watched closely for any sign of the boy, nervous at the prospect of either his presence or absence. As the car slowed toward the duplex, Penny's vision swept across the boy's yard and saw no one on the porch steps. "Well now, I guess I gave that boy the evil eye enough times for him to get the hint," said Mrs. Baker, tapping the ashes from her cigarette out the window. "He's somewhere around," Mr. Baker said. "Count on that. He's always around."

After her lessons were finished, Penny returned to the model car, crumpling the old sheet of wax paper and spreading out a fresh piece to work on. Since the frame was easy to establish, she focused on the smaller pieces, the internals of the automobile. She tilted the lampshade so that more light could hit the desk, and she worked slowly, matching the pieces together, doling out glue in drops so small they seemed invisible. After each fitting, she cracked her knuckles and stretched her arms, enjoying the few seconds before she picked up another piece. Under her breath, she hummed the cheers for tomorrow's game, unsure of the words but positive of the cadence.

A thwacking sound against the window made Penny snap out of her work, causing some of the glue to dribble on her index finger. As quickly as the glue hardened to her skin, another *thwack* bounced off the glass. Penny stepped away from her desk and opened the blinds slowly, a fraction of an inch at each interval. When she could see outside, she peered down at the ground, but nothing was there. She immediately looked toward the boy's house, but he still wasn't there. She was about to shut the blinds when a small acorn bounced off the window, and Penny gasped out loud and jerked away. She immediately felt embarrassed for being surprised and moved closer to pane of glass. She looked to the left, into the tree outside her room, and saw the boy's eyes staring back at her, his mouth open and wide, bright white teeth everywhere. It made Penny dizzy, the sight of him so close, and she began to walk away when she saw him motion with his hand, pointing at her and then the ground. She shook her head. He threw another acorn and smiled. She shook her head again and then closed the blinds.

The model car was waiting but she couldn't concentrate on the pieces, nothing would fit in her clumsy hands, and so she took her book bag into her mother's room and did her homework again, resolving every math problem a second time until she felt calm enough to go work on the car again. When she returned to her room, she began fitting some of the engine parts inside the main frame of the car. After an hour had passed, she went back to the window and looked at the tree but the boy was gone.

∷

On Friday evening, the cheerleaders filed into their own bus, the short bus reserved for handicap students during the school days, to ride over to the away game in Glencliff, an hour and a half away. Until a few years ago, the cheerleaders would ride with the football team, but something unsavory would always happen in the seats at the back of the bus, especially after big wins. The other cheerleaders told Penny about a rumor that the sister of one of the girls in their class had sex with five guys on the team bus after a district playoff game. Penny nodded and widened her eyes and waited for them to talk about something else, her toes balled up inside her sneakers. The girls' conversational patterns would operate in random sequences of the same issues: school, clothes, who is or isn't dating whom, TV, movies and music, and always, without fail, a skillful, quiet shift into sex, the particulars and theoretical. When called upon, Penny had invented three boys in Kingston that she had kissed and one who had wanted to go all the way, but when she refused, told everyone at school that they had. She had to think carefully sometimes to keep the names straight, to avoid the mistake of revealing that she had never touched a boy, did not know what to do with her tongue if she kissed someone, though she had heard several options. Though Penny wasn't so innocent that she never thought of sex, she also could not imagine an actual way that it wouldn't be awkward and unpleasant. In general, sex seemed like chicken pox, inevitable and scarring. And so Penny tried her best to stare out the window, taking part in the easier conversational topics when she could. She did not like away games.

Further along the trip, the senior cheerleaders told everyone what to expect of the Glencliff crowd. "It's mostly blacks and they'll scream at you for the entire game," said Jenny Prince, the captain. "They yelled 'rednecks' at us every time we tried to do a cheer. And some of them started throwing pennies at us, and one hit Marcy Hubbard in the ear and gave her vertigo for the rest of the game." The girls all agreed not to attempt any of the more complex formations. "They get so close to you sometimes," said another senior, "leaning over the fences and trying to grab your hair if you aren't careful. It's always the girls, too." Jenny nodded and said, "Girls are the fucking worst."

The game was as bad as they had been warned. The two football teams were the best in the district and so the game was rough and violent and low-scoring, a cheerleaders' nightmare. One of the Glencliff players hit the Coalfield running back so hard that it sounded like his body had snapped in half, a sharp crack that echoed for a full second afterward. It made Penny wince and look away from the field, toward the crowd, who were smashing their fists into open palms to re-create the sound. When the Glencliff quarterback was sacked and came up clutching his elbow, someone in the bleachers shouted, "You gonna let him get away with that? Kill that motherfucker." Every cheer seemed ridiculous, silly in the face of what was happening on the field. When the cheerleaders shouted, "Take it to them, Chargers!" the crowd shouted back, "Fuck that!" Except for parents of the players and die-hard fans, not many Coalfield fans had come to the game and they seemed reluctant to cheer. Penny thought how stupid team spirit was, how easy it was to kill.

With only a few seconds left to play, the Glencliff team had the ball on Coalfield's three-yard line. This necessitated a cheer, but the girls were hesitant. A Glencliff girl, leaning so hard against the fence that separated the fans from the field that it looked like it would give, yelled, "Say something now, cheer-bitches. Say something now." Suddenly, Jenny Prince spun around and shouted, "Fuck off," which made Penny's face turn hot and red, as embarrassed and shocked as if she had said it herself. The girl against the fence, backed by a half dozen other girls, screamed and shouted obscenities and, by now, most of the other cheerleaders screamed back. Penny just stood there, silent, unsure of how to proceed. One of her pom-poms slipped out of her hand and she made no movement to pick it up. She suddenly remembered every word to the "Push 'em Back" cheer and felt strangely disappointed that there would be no chance to use it. Instead, she mouthed curse words and huddled closer to the other girls, who were now shouting louder than any cheer they had ever done. Suddenly, they heard the crowd groan, and they looked back at the field to see the game had ended and the Coalfield defense had blocked a game-winning field goal attempt. Now the two teams were shoving each other, grabbing facemasks and throwing people to the turf. The cheerleading coach ran to the girls and told them to get to the bus before things got worse.

As the bus drove away, the teams still fighting inside the stadium, a few black girls kept pace with the bus, flipping birds and pounding on the sides of the bus. "This is bad, girls," the cheerleading coach said. "This is dangerous. Just keep the windows closed and crouch down." Penny did as she was told, clutching a bottle of water she had taken from her bag, but the rest of the cheerleaders screamed back at the girls running alongside the bus. "Run over them," said Jenny Prince, and the rest of the girls laughed. Penny turned back toward her window and saw one of the girls looking right at her, smacking the bus and shouting, "Go back home, bitch." Penny felt as if the girl was angry only at her, at something she had specifically done. She wanted to explain that she didn't want to be here either, that she didn't want to be a cheerleader even, but the girl just kept screaming at her. Suddenly Penny opened her window and threw the half-filled water bottle at the girl. It sailed at the girl's head, hitting her just below her left eye and spinning her around, causing her to trip over her own feet and slam onto the pavement, her hands out in front of her. The other cheerleaders were silent for a second and then squealed. Jenny Prince ran over to Penny and gave her a high five. "Oh my God, that was awesome. That was seriously the best thing I've ever seen." Penny still couldn't understand what had happened, felt sick to her stomach, but she was smiling, happy to have made someone else happy.

Penny's mother was waiting for her in the school parking lot when the cheerleaders returned. While the other parents stood in a group, her mother was leaning against the hood of the car, smoking a cigarette and rubbing a strain in her neck. Penny watched her mother notice the bus pulling in, smile, and walk toward the other parents, as if she had been with them the entire time. As Penny and her mother walked to the car, Jenny Prince rushed over to them and said to Penny, "We should celebrate tomorrow. Maybe play some pool at the arcade or something." Penny started to decline, but her mother was standing there with a huge grin, nodding her approval, and so Penny agreed. "Something," she answered. As Jenny Prince ran back to the crowd, Penny's mother said, "Didn't I tell you? I may not have been a cheerleader, but I know they get to have a lot more fun than most people."

Back at the house, Penny's mother dropped her off before she went back to the hospital. "Get inside and relax," she told Penny. "I have to haul rear before anyone knows that my break ended fifteen minutes ago." Once the car pulled away, Penny walked onto the porch and then noticed something on the doormat, shining. She walked closer and saw that it was a model car, a '73 Corvette, cherry red, one she had thrown away several weeks before. She swung around and looked toward the boy's house, but the lights were out. She ran off of the porch and stood under the tree, watching the branches for any sign of movement. When she was satisfied that the boy wasn't around, she walked back to the car and knelt beside it. Inside the car, in the driver's seat, was a piece of paper. She pulled it from the car and smoothed it out on the wood floor of the porch. It simply read: *I really wanna talk to you?*

Upstairs, in her room, Penny read and reread the note. She

rolled the Corvette back and forth along her desk and noticed that the side mirror had snapped off in the garbage. He had gone through her garbage to find this car, and though the idea of it should have unnerved her, made her self-conscious, she wanted to know more about him. She imagined him jumping off his house, the few seconds when he was flying before he was falling. He had to be mentally challenged in some way; why wasn't he in school? And he was at least four years younger than her, a little kid. As she smoothed out the note one more time and wrote on the back of the paper, *Okay,* she felt the ease of her decision and it made her smile.

°°
°°

The next morning, Penny put the car beneath the tree outside her room. She had no idea where else to put it, couldn't leave it on the porch, where her mother would see it, and didn't want to walk into the boy's yard. When the phone rang in the afternoon, she raced to answer it before her mother, fearing that it would be him. Instead it was Jenny Prince, sounding like she always called Penny on Saturday afternoons. "So, you want to cruise around tonight? Robbie's ankle may be broken and he's too depressed to go out tonight, so I thought we could drive around the square and see what's going on." Penny didn't know how to respond. The thought of hanging out with Jenny Prince made her so nervous that for a few seconds, she couldn't say a word. "Hello?" Jenny said. "You still there?" Penny cleared her throat and said, "That's sounds like fun. I don't have a car though." Jenny said that she could pick Penny up and asked where she lived. When Penny told her, Jenny said, "I don't know where that is." Penny explained that it was the little section of houses behind the old refinery, and Jenny paused, thinking, and then said, "Oh, okay. I didn't know anyone lived back there. See you at eight."

Penny's mother was behind her when she hung up the phone. "I trust you to have fun without getting into trouble," she said. "Be smart." Penny nodded and then looked out the window. The car was still beneath the tree.

By that evening, Penny had nearly finished the Pontiac GTO. After each new addition, she waited for the glue to bond and then carefully swept her index finger over the frame, memorizing the lines of the car. When her mother knocked on the door, Penny was surprised at how late it was. She went to the window to look for the car, but her mother walked in and Penny whirled around to meet her. "I'm going to work," her mother said. "Call me at the hospital if something comes up. Be home by midnight. I'll be home after that."

When Penny returned to the window, she saw that the Corvette was gone. She looked into the tree and saw the boy, holding the car in his hand, smiling. Penny put a finger to her lips, to silence him, and waited for her mother to drive away. Then Penny opened the window and the boy said, "Do you know where the storage shed is? The one next to the refinery?" Penny nodded. "Come over there," he said. Penny nodded again and there was silence. The boy coughed and said, "Some kids go there to make out."

Penny said, "I'm not going to make out with you."

"You don't have to," he said, "I just want to talk to you."

Penny called Jenny Prince and told her that she couldn't go out. "My neighbor has an emergency and I have to babysit her kid," she told Jenny.

"God, that's stupid," said Jenny, "just say you can't." Penny said that she had to and Jenny finally sighed and said, "Okay, but you have to do something next weekend. Promise?" Penny promised and hung up, then put on her jacket and a knit cap and started walking to the storage shed. She picked up a piece of wood and swung at the weeds beside the road that led to the shed. Walking slowly, her breath clouding in front of her, her heartbeat was steady, though she knew that she was supposed to be nervous.

The boy was already there, leaning against the wall of the shed, making a lighter spark without creating a flame. When he saw Penny, he straightened up and put the lighter in his pocket. He was wearing a scarf around his neck, which hid the lower part of his face, but he still wasn't wearing shoes. He picked the car up off of the ground and held it out to her. She shook her head and he frowned, then put it back down on the ground.

"Where did you get that car?" she asked him.

He looked at the car and seemed to be concentrating, trying to remember. "I found it," he said.

"Yeah," she said, "but where did you find it?"

"I didn't know that girls liked cars."

Penny laughed and then said, "I don't like them. I like models. I don't care about cars."

"Well, I don't like them either."

"Okay," she said.

"Okay."

There was silence. There was a beeping sound from a truck backing up but it was several blocks away. Penny listened to it and tapped her foot in time to the sound.

"How old are you?" he asked.

"Sixteen," she said. "How old are you?"

The boy looked at the car again. "I read at a high school level."

"But how old are you?"

"Twelve."

Penny walked near him and picked the car up off of the ground. The note was still there.

"Why did you want to talk to me?" she asked him.

"Because I just did," he said.

"Well, I have to go back home. I don't want you going through our things. I don't want you to watch me from the tree either."

The boy frowned again. "I won't then."

"Okay then."

"But can I talk to you again?"

"Why?"

His eyes became very small, almost slits. He looked like he was going to cry and Penny wished very hard that he wouldn't. He untied his scarf and held the ends of it in either hand.

"My grandma takes care of me. She teaches me at home because she doesn't want me to go to school with everybody. I don't like it. I thought maybe we could see each other every once in a while."

Penny realized that she was still holding the Corvette in her hands and she walked over to the boy and handed it to him. He took the note out of the car and put it in his jacket pocket.

"I'll put the car back in the trash where I found it," he said. "I won't mess around with your stuff anymore."

Penny took the car again and shifted it back and forth between her hands.

"I'll keep it. And sometimes, I can put the car under the tree and then we can meet here again. Sometimes."

The boy smiled and then nodded. "I won't go back in the tree either. I won't go up in it and watch you."

"Okay then."

"Show me one of those cheers," he said. "You're a cheerleader, right? I see you wearing the outfit sometimes."

"I don't know any of the cheers. I can't remember them."

"Can you do a cartwheel or a flip or something?"

She looked around at the ground. There were rusted cans and cigarette butts near her feet.

"There might be glass. I don't think I should."

"If I show you something, will you?"

"Maybe," she said.

He reached into one of his pockets and took out a small white packet. Penny walked closer to him. It was a packet of nondairy creamer. "Watch," he said. "Watch this." He sprinkled the powder into the palm of his hand and then took out his lighter. He held the flame to his hand and the powder flashed and a bright white flame ran across his hand. Penny gasped, but the boy just laughed and then shook his hand. "It doesn't hurt," he said. "Watch." He touched her hand and she let him pour a packet of the creamer into her palm. "Be still," he said, and flicked the lighter. The same flash happened and she felt the instant rush of heat spread across her palm and then disappear. She was turning her hand over, holding it close to her face, when he leaned in and asked, "It didn't hurt?" She shook her head and smiled. "I told you," he said.

The boy was staring at her, his head tilted to the side like a dog trying to understand an unfamiliar command. Penny looked away, tucked her chin under her shoulder. She felt his hand on her arm and before she could turn toward him, it was gone. His head tilted to the other side and Penny felt the cold starting to sink under her skin. She pushed away from the shed and the boy called out, "Are you leaving?" She nodded and walked a little farther and then stopped. She turned toward him and quickly did a standing backflip. She landed a little to one side and hobbled a few steps to the left, but the boy whistled.

"Can you teach me to do that?" he asked.

"I'll put the car out under the tree next time," she said.

As she walked through the weeds, she heard him say, "Soon."

∞

Penny assembled the GTO just before her mother came. Finishing a car always made her happy, and the meeting with the boy outside in the cold had made her face pink and shiny. So when her mother quietly knocked on the door and then walked in, it must have seemed like Penny was finally understanding the benefits of being a cheerleader.

"You had fun?" she asked Penny.

"I did," Penny said. "I hadn't expected to, but I did."

Her mother walked over and pulled her close to her. "I knew it even when you didn't. I knew you would have fun. Are you going out again with the other girls?"

"Next week."

Penny felt her happiness fading, and it made her ashamed that this was happening. She often wished that the things that made her happy were the same things that made her mother happy. She thought about next weekend and could not picture what it would be like. And then she thought about the boy, his strange baby face that she wanted to stare at but she was embarrassed to look too closely. Finally, her mother glanced at her watch and said, "I better get to sleep. It was a long night. Guy got his hand caught in a garbage disposal. It's never the clean cuts that you hope for, just jagged, mangled messes."

As soon as her mother left, Penny crawled under the covers and pretended to be asleep until she finally was.

⠿

When Penny awoke in the morning, she put on her jacket over her pajamas, slipped into a pair of sneakers, and crept down the stairs, past her mother, still asleep, and walked out the front door, Corvette in hand. She stood under the tree and touched the bark with her free hand, making sure no one was around. She swept aside a few leaves and placed the car so that it was facing the boy's house, the chrome grille pointing directly toward his front door.

Back in her room, she picked up her desk chair and moved it in front of the window. She reached into her book bag and retrieved a book for English. She held the book just below her line of vision, and watched the tree. Pretty soon, her arms grew tired. She paced in circles around the room, stopping at the window every time. Finally, she changed into jeans and a sweater and left a note for her mother—*Walking. Love, me*—and went outside, heading toward the storage shed, the sun just rising over the horizon.

The boy arrived less than fifteen minutes later, his hair uncombed, still barefoot. He was holding the car with both hands, held out in front of him like he was presenting her with a gift. He placed the car beside her feet and then leaned against the wall, standing shoulder to shoulder with Penny.

"You showed up fast," she said.

"I had to finish my breakfast with my grandma before she would let me go outside."

"Where are your parents?"

He slid down the wall until he was sitting on the ground. She followed him. She wanted to rest her head on his shoulder, but she didn't.

"I don't know where they are," he said. "Somewhere."

"You don't know where?"

"My mom is in Alabama, working somewhere. I don't know who my dad is. I've never met him, I mean."

"My dad is back in Kingston, where we used to live," she told him, though he didn't seem to be listening.

After a few minutes of silence, feet scratching against the gravel, he said, "Do you miss him?"

"No," she said, shocked at her own words. Then she realized it was true and she said it again. "No, I don't miss him," and this time it sounded fine.

"I don't either," he said. "They can stay gone."

Neither of them said anything for a while. The boy took out his lighter again and flicked it on and off, while Penny watched his face, the calm, almost bored way that he regarded the flame. She couldn't think of anything to say; she never knew if the other person wanted to hear what she had to say, so she bit her lip and wished there was something specific she could ask, something interesting. She wished she had her own lighter to play with, something for her hands to hold, and so she picked up the model car and held it until something came to her.

"My neighbors," Penny said, "the Bakers—"

"They don't like me," he said, still flicking the lighter.

"How do you know?"

"I know."

"Well, they said that you jumped off your house."

"I did."

"Why?"

"I wanted to try something out. It didn't work, but I kinda thought it wouldn't. I still wanted to try it though. I'm not that interested in flying anymore. I don't have the materials I need yet. I need lots of things I can't get."

"So maybe you'll try it again?"

"Yeah, and it'll work the next time."

Penny nodded and the boy stared at her for a long time. He frowned and then looked down at his feet.

"You think it's stupid?" he asked her.

"I don't know. I guess not. No more stupid than anything else."

He touched her cheek with the back of his hand. It was warm against her face. She leaned into him and though she didn't look at him, she knew he wanted to kiss her and so she closed her eyes and let him. She felt his mouth against her cheek and when she didn't say anything, he kissed her again. When she opened her eyes, his face was so close to hers that it felt like she was fighting for air with him, passing it back and forth, and then she pulled on his shirt until his mouth was touching hers. He tasted like sugary cereal and his lips were soft and smooth against hers. She felt his tongue lick at her teeth, which she did not like, made her think of the dentist. So she closed her mouth and he instantly stopped and waited for her to kiss him again, which she did, over and over until it was understandable, something she could remember later.

∷

In the cafeteria on Monday, the other cheerleaders were still talking about the Glencliff game. Jenny Prince kept reenacting the moment when she yelled at the girl behind the fence. Each time she spun around and yelled, "Fuck off," the other girls giggled and shook their heads. Penny kept eating her sandwich, thinking about the girl she had hit with the bottle. She knew it would be mentioned, but she hoped she would not have to re-create the event. A group of football players walked by with their trays of food, stopping for a second to lean over the girls. Spencer Ivey, who had blocked the final field goal attempt, lifted his shirt and showed them an enormous purple bruise that started at his armpit and went all the way down to his waist. He then pointed to Penny and said, "I heard you bruised up somebody too." Jenny Prince stood up and told Spencer the story once more, spinning around on one foot and then throwing her hands out in front of her. "We could use a backup quarterback with your throwing arm," he said, and then picked up his tray and followed the rest of the boys to their own table. After they were gone, the girls were all looking at Penny, smiling. Her sandwich was finished, her tray empty, and she fought the urge to pick something off another girl's tray so that she could avoid talking. "What do you think of Spencer?" one of the girls asked. Penny shrugged her shoulders and then shook her carton of milk to see if any was left. "Well, he's your date after the game on Friday," said Jenny Prince, and the other girls hooted loudly, which made Penny's face color and her hands shake just slightly. She wished she had a model car in front of her to calm her nerves. And then she thought of the boy, his mouth, and her hands shook so hard that she knocked over her empty carton of milk.

Penny's mother had the night off, and it was nearly midnight before Penny was able to place the Corvette under the tree. She looked across the street and noticed a faint light coming from the room at the far corner of the boy's house. As she walked toward the storage shed, out of the corner of her eye, she saw the light go dim, but she did not turn around to watch, simply put one foot in front of the other until she was touching the metal wall of the shed. And when she turned around, the boy was there, smiling at her. "I wasn't going to sleep until I saw it," he said. "I'd have stayed awake all night."

This time, they made out first, standing up, leaning against the wall. Even though he was twelve, he was only an inch shorter than Penny, and she liked the way their bodies lined up. She was worried that he would want to do more, to touch her under her clothes, but he never tried, seemed as amazed as Penny that any of this was happening. When they finally stopped, Penny and the boy sat down on the gravel and watched the clouds pass over the moon.

"You're real pretty," he said.

"I'm not," Penny said. She did not like people telling her that she was pretty because it meant they were looking at her.

"Yeah, you are. And you're nice."

"That's 'cause you're real nice to me," Penny said, and kissed him just below his left eye, which made him blink a few times and then yawn. With his mouth wide open, it seemed like the rest of his features disappeared behind it, and she thought again of how strange his face was, which pleased her. When she was away from him, it made it easy to picture him; the specifics were so easy to remember. When he finished yawning, he looked up at her and smiled.

"What?" he asked.

"You're real pretty too."

°°

For the rest of the week, Jenny Prince tried harder to include Penny in the conversations at the lunch table. "You're a badass," she told Penny. "You passed the test." Penny was chewing her food so slowly at lunch that her teeth ached down to the gums. Spencer kept lingering at the table as he walked by, resting his tray near Penny's, always hovering over her. He asked her to help him with his Algebra II homework. Penny stammered and then said, "You can just copy mine," which made him laugh loudly. "I like this girl," he said. "She makes it a lot easier than it should be." When he walked away, Carrie Cunningham said, "He really likes you." Penny looked down at her tray and said, "Okay." Jenny Prince nudged her until she looked up at her. "Just don't make it that easy on Friday night," she said, but softly, so no one else could hear, and Penny was grateful for that much.

In the car, on the way home, Mrs. Baker turned around in her seat and faced Penny. "That boy still troubling you?" she asked. Penny shook her head. "You always quiet," Mrs. Baker said, taking a slow drag on her cigarette, "but last couple days, you been quiet in a way that makes me think you got more going on." Penny blushed and looked at the window. "Boyfriend," Mrs. Baker said instantly, "you got a boyfriend. Easy." She smiled, pleased with herself, and turned around in her seat. She tapped her husband on his shoulder and said, "Boyfriend," and her husband nodded, still staring ahead.

∞

After school, she rushed through her homework, not entirely caring if she got the right answers, and then paced around her room until she could put the car under the tree. Sometimes the Bakers would stay on the porch, finishing their cigarettes, and she had to be careful that they didn't see her. She hardly ever looked at the GTO anymore, and she was too nervous to start another. She was filled with so much energy that she started practicing her cheers and she found that the movements came easier to her, that the accumulation of pep rallies and games and practices had sunk into her muscles and stayed there.

When she finally got away, she waited at the shed, blowing warm air into her fists, and she could feel her body getting lighter, the things she kept inside her turning to air. She pretended that a comet had hit the earth and that she was the only person left in the world. And then, suddenly, rustling in the high weeds, another person, one other person still alive, carrying a model car in his hands like it was a small animal.

"We're the only people left, everyone else is dead," she said after they had stopped making out. He took out a small canister of breath spray and sprayed it into the flame of his lighter, making a flamethrower. "I can make fire, then," he said and Penny was so delighted that he had understood, had not made her feel strange, that she leaned into him and kissed him again.

$$\underset{\circ}{\circ}\underset{\circ}{\circ}$$

On Friday night, Penny could actually remember a few of the cheers and it surprised her to hear her own voice shouting in unison with the other girls. She wondered if everything was like this, that you pretend you know something until you do. The Chargers were winning easily, already twenty-one points ahead in the second quarter and so the cheerleaders had to do little to keep the crowd happy. A hopeful Hail Mary pass was lofted toward the receiver that Spencer was covering. Penny watched the tight spiral of the ball and when she looked at the intended receiver, she noticed that he was all alone. Behind the play, Spencer was on the ground, stumbling to get back up. The receiver easily caught the pass and ran into the end zone, Spencer trailing by ten yards. When he returned to the sidelines, the coach slapped him on the back of his helmet, and she saw his shoulders hunch as if he expected more. "He's thinking about you," said Jenny. "Can't focus on the game."

Just before halftime, Penny saw the boy in the stands. At first, she thought she was imagining it, but there he was, in the first row, arms hanging over the metal rail, almost leaning off his seat. He lifted one of his arms and waved and she instinctively did the same, the pom-pom in her hand brushing against her cheek. Beside the boy was someone Penny assumed was his grandmother. She was sitting upright, back straight, reading a book. She looked younger than Penny had imagined, more capable. The boy would not stop staring at her.

During the halftime show, Penny felt so distracted by the boy's presence that she almost dropped Misty Grubbs during a particularly difficult basket catch. After the show, the cheerleading coach hissed at Penny, "Keep your head in the game. Can't look bad at home and you're making us look bad." Jenny Prince came over to her and said, "No one cares."

After the game, the boy caught up to Penny as she was walking toward the gym, to change in the girls' locker room. She broke out of the group of cheerleaders and waited for him. "You are a good cheerleader," he said. "You know all them cheers. My grandma thinks I'm in the restroom." He had a piece of popcorn caught in the tangles of his hair and she pulled it out. "Somebody was throwing popcorn at me," he said. "I acted like I didn't notice but that made them throw more." The other cheerleaders were turning their heads now toward Penny and the boy, though they kept walking to the gym. "Can we do something tonight?" he asked. "Can you put the car out later?" She almost said yes, the wanting of it nearly forcing the word out of her, but then remembered her plans. "I have to go out with some people now," she said.

"Who with?" he asked.

"Just people from school," she said. She said she'd put the car out in the morning and they could meet then, but she knew he was disappointed.

"I came to see you tonight," he told her. "I begged my grandma until she let me." He moved closer to her but she knew people were watching; she hated being watched, and so she turned toward the gym.

"Tomorrow morning," she said, "I promise." She kept walking and didn't turn around until she was at the entrance to the gym and when she turned around, he was still standing there.

"Who is that kid?" asked Jenny Prince, who seemed annoyed by the boy's presence.

"My neighbor," said Penny. "The one I babysit sometimes."

Once they had showered and changed, the girls waited for the football team to come out of the locker room. Spencer was the last one to appear and his hair was still wet, his head down. Jenny said that Penny should ride with Spencer to the party and Penny couldn't think of a way to say no, merely stood in place until Spencer walked beside her and nodded to the parking lot, not meeting her eyes.

In the car, Spencer turned on the radio to a classic rock station and then switched it off just as quickly. Penny looked out the window of the passenger side, trying to think of something to say, hoping she wouldn't have to say anything. "I don't want to go to that party," Spencer said. "I don't feel like partying." He pulled into a fast food parking lot and stopped the car. Penny knew she had to say something but what she wanted was to get out of the car and walk home. He seemed petulant and childish to her, just because he messed up one play. Then she began to wonder if he even liked football, if he was only on the team because someone made him. She turned to tell him that at least the team won, but he was already leaning into her, reaching for her. He kissed her, his tongue in her mouth, and she kept trying to spit it out. He reached for the bottom of her shirt, but she put her hand on the edge to keep him from pulling it up. As quickly as it had happened, he pulled away from her and put both of his hands on the wheel. "I think I better go home," Penny said.

Spencer nodded and then said, "I'm having an off night. I'm better than this usually." He looked over at her for the first time all night and it looked like he was about to cry.

"I better go home," she said again, and he started the car.

"Don't tell anyone about this," he said as he drove her home.

"No," she answered. She could not imagine how she would explain it to anyone.

"I didn't know anyone lived back here," he said, as he pulled onto her street.

"Well," he said, "bye." He wouldn't look at her and she felt so embarrassed about what had happened in the parking lot that she simply stepped out of the car and kept walking. Her mother was at the hospital so at least she wouldn't have to explain why she was home so early. As she got to her door, she heard the car's tires squeal as Spencer spun out of her neighborhood.

Mrs. Baker came to her door and walked onto the porch and saw Penny. She pointed to the taillights of the disappearing car and said, "Boyfriend?" Penny shook her head. "That's good," Mrs. Baker said. "That's very good," and then she walked back inside. Penny looked across the street and saw that the boy's room was dark.

As Penny was brushing her teeth, the thought of Spencer's tongue made her gag. She suddenly imagined that Spencer would go to the party after all, make up a story about her and him in the parking lot. She thought of how probable this event was, so much so that she tried to anticipate what she would say when the other girls asked her about it at lunch on Monday. She couldn't think of anything. She felt sad at how often she believed that something was going to turn out badly and how she was almost always right. She finished brushing her teeth and went back to her room, where acorns were bouncing off her window.

She opened the window and peered down to see the boy, standing under the tree. "I didn't want to wait until tomorrow," he said. She put a finger to her lips to quiet him, but he kept talking. "Was that your boyfriend?" She shook her head. "Am I your boyfriend?" he asked. She didn't move. She didn't know what to say. He took out his lighter and then whispered, "Well, I wish I was." She told him that she would meet him at the storage shed later, but he shook his head. "I made something for you," he said. "You can see it from there. You don't have to move." She saw a can of gasoline by the tree and she was afraid he was going to set it on fire. "Don't," she said, but then he knelt down, facing away from the tree, and touched the lighter to the grass in the front yard. A ball of fire kicked up into the air and then Penny saw the boy stumble backward, waving his arms in front of him. The ground beside him slowly filled with flames, moving and bending in a single line. In the second it took for the flame to reach the end of its line, she realized that it spelled out her name, her own name in fire on the front lawn. And then she saw the boy, on his back, his right arm encased in flames.

She clamped her hand over her mouth to muffle her screams but she wasn't screaming, wasn't making a sound. She turned and ran down the stairs, out onto the porch, and into the yard, where the boy was now standing on his feet, rotating his arm in circles. She ran into him and the force of the collision sent them onto the ground, where she immediately started slapping at the flame. She could feel the heat on her hands, all the way up her neck and to the top of her head, but it wouldn't go out. The boy was not making a sound, though she saw that his mouth was wide open, as if he were yawning. He was looking at her, but she could only focus on the fire, which would not stop, no matter how hard she tried to put it out. Then she felt something pull her off the boy and she saw Mr. Baker quickly wrap the boy up and roll him around on the ground. She wanted to stay close, but someone else had her now, hands slapping against her head, and then she realized her hair had been on fire. Penny couldn't feel anything but the smell made her nauseous and she sat up on her knees and tried to throw up but she couldn't make herself.

Mrs. Baker was now pulling Penny to the car, opening the door and pushing her into the backseat. The boy was already in the back, lying down, and Penny lifted his head and slid underneath it, letting him rest in her lap. She touched his forehead with her fingers but her hands were swollen and she couldn't feel his skin. His burned arm was hanging off the seat, his fingers touching the floorboard, but she didn't look. She just kept staring at him, his eyes still open and focused on her, and waited for something good to happen, for things to be better than they seemed.

At the hospital, the orderlies wheeled the boy through the doors and into the emergency room. Penny was not allowed to go with him, was forced to wait for another doctor to look at her. She sat in the waiting room with the Bakers, who had yet to say a single word to Penny. Mr. Baker just kept shaking his head and Mrs. Baker would put her hand on the back of his neck until he stopped. Penny felt fine, but her hands were bright red and swollen to nearly twice their size. She was embarrassed because it seemed like the entire waiting room smelled of her burned hair. An older man was sitting across from her, holding his stomach and rocking back and forth, and she caught him staring at her head several times. After a few minutes, Penny's mother came running into the waiting room and when she saw Penny, she said, "Oh, honey, are you okay? Your hair." She touched Penny's shoulders and turned her first one way and then the other, checking her skin for burns. "Let me go talk to the nurse and get someone to look at you right away," she said, and ran to the desk. Mrs. Baker rubbed Penny's back and said, "That boy will be okay. Mr. Baker got the fire out. And you will be fine too. Everything will be fine, baby." Mr. Baker started to shake his head again and this time Mrs. Baker pinched his shoulder to make him stop.

The doctor put burn cream, bright white and thick, on her hands and on the left side of her neck. "You're lucky the fire didn't reach your scalp," the doctor said, "that would have been unpleasant." When he was finished, Penny asked her mother if she could stay until the boy was okay, but her mother said, "His grandmother is here, and we need to go home. You need to sleep and then we'll think of something to do about your hair." When they walked into the waiting room, she saw the boy's grandmother, sitting as straight as she was at the football game, her hair disheveled and the light blue fabric of a nightgown peeking out from underneath her dress. She did not look at Penny, would not turn her head, but kept staring straight ahead, silent.

Penny slept with her mother that night, her hands inside plastic Ziploc bags to keep the cream from rubbing on the sheets. Her mother kept her arm draped over Penny, and whenever Penny awoke during the night, it took her several seconds to remember what had happened, why she was in bed with her mother. She had a fitful dream where the boy was gathering brushwood to build a fire. He would not speak to her, simply pulled more and more wood into a pile until it seemed like it was going to topple over, a tower of wood, but Penny awoke to the sunlight filling the room before he could set it on fire.

Penny's hands were less swollen now, the skin on the back peeling and itching, but she could feel the texture of the sheets when she touched them. She rubbed the left side of her head and heard the crunching sound of her burned hair, pieces of it falling into her lap. Her mother was still asleep and Penny stood up and walked into the bathroom. When she looked in the mirror, it did not look like her at all. The left side of her head was burned to a little less than an inch of hair. She started to cry and then decided it wasn't worth the effort. She reached into the drawer that held her mother's scissors and began cutting handfuls of hair from the right side of her head, letting it fall in a pile around her feet. Then she took the clippers that her mother had used to cut her father's hair and put on the attachment that would provide the closest trim. She started on the burned side and pulled the clippers slowly from front to back. Yellow wisps of hair clung to her face but she kept going. By the time she had finished the left side, she heard her mother stirring from sleep. She worked quickly on the right side and when her mother walked into the bathroom, she gasped, as if the breath had been kicked out of her, and took the clippers out of Penny's hands, who did not resist. She could tell her mother was going to cry, and was surprised when she didn't. Her mother simply touched Penny's face, turning her from side to side as she watched the reflection in the mirror. "That's fine," her mother said, trying to smile. "That's fine." When Penny looked at herself, she was quietly happy to see that she liked how she appeared. Her eyes seemed bigger, wider, and she liked the shape of her ears now that there was no hair to cover them. She looked boyish, yes, but pretty, and she kept staring at herself until she was entirely convinced that it was still her, the same person. Penny touched the smoothness of her head and saw her mother's reflection shudder.

For three days, Penny did not see the boy. Her mother would only say, "He's better, but he's in trouble. He damaged property and could have hurt people." Just knowing that he was okay was enough, allowed Penny to feel hopeful. Her mother had allowed her to miss school for the week, and she stayed in her bed until her mother went to work. Once she heard the car pull away, Penny sat in front of the window and watched the boy's house. The grass in Penny's front yard was scorched black and seemed to spell out *Pomy*, but she could still picture it as it first looked, bluish-white and rippling against the wind.

When she was convinced that he wasn't home, she went to the closet and got another model, a 1961 Cobra that had real leather seats. She had been saving it for a special occasion but her hands were still sore and it was difficult to fit the pieces together. She got so frustrated that she dumped it into the trash. She pulled her chair back to the window and waited.

Late that afternoon, she saw Jenny Prince's car pull up to her house. Penny leaned close to the window and watched Jenny slowly walk up to the porch, staring from the Bakers' door back to Penny's, trying to decide which doorbell to ring. Penny started to climb into bed, pretend to be asleep, but she stopped and put on some clothes, started to pull her hair back into a ponytail and instead felt the fuzz atop her head. She reached for a knit cap and ran down the stairs. When Jenny saw her, she said, "Take off the hat," and smiled when she saw Penny's new haircut. "It suits you," she said. "Very badass." Penny stepped onto the porch and saw the armful of books that Jenny was holding. "Homework," Jenny told her. "So you don't flunk out."

Penny took the books, thanked her, and then said, "Can you drive me to the hospital?"

In the car, Penny told Jenny Prince about the boy, everything. Jenny whistled and then said, "That's not so bad. I made out with some guy in my dad's firm. At least with you, no one goes to jail."

"Why have you been so nice to me lately?" asked Penny.

"Well, you're nice, even though you're quiet and kind of weird. You don't act all stupid and fake. I don't know. Don't you want me to be nice to you?"

"I guess," said Penny. "I just wondered. I'm quitting the cheerleading squad."

"That's fine," Jenny said. "You didn't have much spirit anyways."

∷

At the hospital, when Penny tried to see the boy, the nurse went to his room and returned with the boy's grandmother close behind. "Come here," she said to Penny and then walked to a couple of chairs in the waiting room. She looked at Penny for a long time, but Penny was too scared to look away. "How old are you?" the woman asked.

"Sixteen."

"And you know my grandson is twelve?"

"Yes, ma'am."

"Don't you find that strange? That someone your age would be interested in someone like my grandson?"

"Yes, ma'am. It seems strange."

"It *is* strange. I know my grandson is mature for his age. He's smart and charming and enthusiastic, but he is still twelve. My grandson likes you very much. He's very taken with you and seems to think that you like him."

"I do. I mean, I think he's very nice."

"Well, I want to tell you that my grandson is very taken with lots of things. He was very taken with flying and airplanes and then he was very taken with fire, and I'm sure he's very taken with you. But he will be taken with something else soon and hopefully it will be less dangerous than flying and fire and sixteen-year-old girls. Of course, I want him to have friends. I would like him to have people who care about him and appreciate what a special person he is, but I also would like it very much if you could help him find something else to be taken with. I would like you to do that as quickly as you can. Do you understand me?"

"Yes, ma'am."

"Good."

"Can I talk to him?"

"No, I don't think so. Let's give him a chance to find something in the hospital that he could be taken with."

"Okay, I understand."

When the boy's grandmother stood up, she smiled at Penny, thin and quick, and then walked back down the hallway. Penny watched her leave and then realized that her mother might see her and quickly walked out of the hospital.

∷

Two days later, the boy came back home. Penny saw his grandmother's car pull into the driveway. As the grandmother opened the passenger door, the boy's right arm, bandaged and bright white, poked out of the car, and the sight of it made Penny's stomach sink. She saw the boy's face as he walked around the car, toward the front door, and he looked up at the window, his eyes squinting to find her. She waved quickly and then backed away before his grandmother could see.

Penny and her mother ate dinner together that night, which they were unaccustomed to and Penny was constantly surprised to see her mother across the table from her. As they washed dishes, Penny's mother cleared her throat, then cleared it again, and said, "I talked to your father today."

"Oh," said Penny, rubbing a towel over a dish long after it was dry.

"We don't like each other," her mother said. "I especially don't like him, but we agree about a few things and one of them is that we are worried about you. You can understand why."

"I guess."

"We want you to talk to someone. A professional. At least for a little while."

"I really don't want to," said Penny. The thought of a person who was paid money just to focus on nothing but her for an hour made her sick.

"Well, we want you to do it. Pen, I don't think you really appreciate the good in your life. You are always so unhappy. And I don't pretend that this is a great situation, living in a strange place with all the stress of the divorce and fitting in at school. But you are pretty and kind and you had the opportunity to make the best of this situation and you just refused to do it. I try and try to steer you toward good things and you run in the opposite direction and that hurts me."

"I don't like what you think is good. I don't like cheerleading and school and other people."

"Oh, I know that," said her mother. "I'll learn to live with that. I won't be happy at first and it'll hurt my feelings for a while, but I guess that's what I have to accept."

"Thank you," said Penny, not knowing what else to say.

"Don't say that," said her mother, who was now crying. "Don't pretend that either one of us is happy with the other."

Penny placed the dish in the cabinet and looked at her mother. She wanted to hug her, to touch her, but she walked up the stairs and closed her bedroom door behind her.

∞

Penny waited until long after she was sure that her mother was asleep before she walked down the steps and out of the house. It was three in the morning, and the moon was less than a thumbnail of light in the sky, but Penny was still afraid of being seen. She ran across the street and hid between the wall of the boy's house, just under his window, and a bare rose bush. She peered in the window but couldn't see anything, even with the faint glow of a nightlight shimmering in the room. She hunkered down beneath the window for a few seconds and then popped up again, this time staring a little longer, allowing her eyes to adjust to the darkness. She could finally see the boy, in bed, arm held up by a little metal pulley that was nailed to the ceiling. His grandmother was not in the room. Penny scratched on the frame of the window, afraid that even that small amount of noise would lead to her discovery. The boy did not rouse. She watched his face, the calm, perfect way he took air into and out of his body. She tapped lightly on the window but still nothing. Finally, a steady tapping, the insistent Morse code of the tip of her finger against glass, and his eyes opened. She almost shouted when she saw the small slits of his eyes, but managed to just keep tapping, tapping, until he located the sound. When he saw her, Penny waved, and he tried to wave back but his arm clanked against the pulley. He winced and then carefully maneuvered his arm out of the sling. He crawled over to the window and opened it with his good arm, slowly, careful not to make too much noise. Once it was opened enough for her hands to reach under, she raised the window the rest of the way. She dug her shoes into the cracks of the brick wall and pulled herself inside, softly sliding into the room until she was lying on her back, staring up at the boy, who was staring at her hair, touching her head with his finger. He was nodding, and so she did the same.

She slipped out of her pants, the cold attaching itself to the skin of her legs, and carefully shifted her weight onto the bed, careful to avoid noise. She started to help the boy slide back into the sling, but he shook his head. They lay on the bed, shoulder to shoulder, silent until the boy turned his head to her and said, "Are you mad at me?" She shook her head. "I ruined everything," he said but she shook her head again. She kissed him and he kissed her back and they were silent for a long time.

"Is your arm okay?" she asked.

"They had to take skin from my leg. It's going to look weird. But I'm okay. I'm always okay. I get hurt but it never hurts much."

"It was scary," she said, shuddering from the memory of it.

"It's harder to watch, I bet, than it is to do it."

"I don't think so," she said, and pointed to his arm.

"I like you so much," he said. "I really do like you so much." Penny said, "I like you too. I like you so much too."

"Can we be friends, still?" he asked. "No matter what?"

She loved him and she couldn't explain exactly why and this made her think that it must be true. He rubbed his head against hers and then said, "Watch this."

He lifted the covers and swiftly rubbed his feet up and down the fabric of the bedsheets. After a few seconds, under the covers, tiny sparks of static electricity shot across the bed, jumping around like fireflies. Penny made the same motion with her feet and watched even more sparks lift and hover in the air. They giggled and even though she knew that she would have to leave soon, she felt the closeness of the boy against her and watched the sparks light up and die out, over and over, until the two of them became still, and it was dark and quiet and perfect once again.

the museum of whatnot

A man himself is junk and all his life he clutters the earth with it . . . he lives in it. He loves it. He worships it. He collects it and stands guard over it.

—WILLIAM SAROYAN, 1952

this is how my day starts: checking the newspaper hats for silverfish. Dusting the mason jars of baby teeth. Realigning the framed labels of apricot jars. My mother calls me every Friday to remind me about my body. "Janey, you're going to wake up one day, childless, and all you'll have are those . . . things." And probably she's right. Still, I tell her that I'd rather watch over other people's useless things than have to deal with my own. She hangs up after that.

I am thirty-one years old. I have a degree in Museum Science from Dartmouth. I keep to myself. I am the caretaker and sole employee of the Carl Jensen Museum of Whatnot. We, and by we, I mean me, call it the MOW. We sell T-shirts but no one's buying.

The MOW is the only museum in the world dedicated solely to the acquisition and preservation of the everyday made unique. Things that are ordinarily junk but not junk because someone, somewhere, made it more than that by their collecting, hoarding, and preserving it.

In 1927, Carl Jensen passed away and, as is the custom when rich people die without heirs, he had decided that the house he'd lived in would be made available to the public. However, Mr. Jensen had no art collection to speak of, no gold-leaf furniture, no snuffboxes from China. What he did have was five hundred and seventy-three framed labels of canned apricots, apricots that none of his closest friends had ever heard him admit a fondness for. He also had a stipulation in his will that his estate be turned into a museum to house not only his own collection of artifacts, but also those of other like-minded people. And that is why I am sitting here in this echoing house, taking care of inanimate objects that someone cared for with more passion and tenderness than I have ever felt about anything, animal, vegetable, or mineral.

⁛

I was just out of grad school, working part-time at a second-rate museum of history at a state university, and living with a man who was writing a novel about bird-watchers. Flipping through the pages of *Curator Monthly,* I found a classified that asked for someone in the field of museum arts who was willing to veer off the beaten path. Up to this point, all I knew were beaten paths, tattooed with footprints, and I had come to the understanding that they were not much fun to travel because so many people were waiting for you at the end, wondering what took you so long. So, three interviews later, conducted with the very aged board of directors, all collectors of knickknackery who were ensuring that their collections would live on, I was hired. I quit my job, packed my very few belongings, left the man and his typewriter and Audubon books, and moved into an apartment on the third floor of the mansion. It was just me and the stuff. I bounced a ball off the steps of the giant staircase. I played hide-and-seek by myself, sitting for hours behind a curtain. I drank a lot of bourbon. After a week, I realized I was going crazy, and decided I'd better put the ball and alcohol away and start dusting.

⁛

Here are the comment cards in the Suggestion Box for the month of April:

> Weird.
>
> This place is really weird.
>
> A very curious place. I will recommend this to my friends.
>
> Nice place but the art is really weird.
>
> I am very disappointed. My stepdaughter cried when she saw the chicken bones exhibit.
>
> Why am I supposed to care about these things? Tell me that.
>
> Weird!
>
> A snack bar would be nice.
>
> Weird
>
> Get a fucking life.

As for me, I don't keep anything. The only thing I own outright, not provided by the estate, is a transistor radio that on good days can pick up stations in Eastern Europe. Anytime in my life when I see an accumulation of items, a title of ownership in my name, I feel my insides swell. What am I going to do with all of this? Where am I going to put it? So I get rid of it. And I feel calm again. I am a library patron, a renter without an option to buy, a Salvation Army donator, a spring cleaner of the highest order.

Why then, why in the world, do I work here, surrounded by all of this? It's easy enough. This is art, and it is not mine. I am only looking after it while the real owners are away. Most of all, I suppose, although I may not want things, I don't mind touching them for a while.

$$\vcenter{\hbox{$\bullet\bullet$}}\atop\vcenter{\hbox{$\bullet\bullet$}}$$

It is Wednesday afternoon, which is why the doctor is here. He is a regular, one of those whom I can count on no matter how few people step inside the museum each week. He comes in every Wednesday during lunch hour, white coat on, stethoscope around his neck. I look up from my library book and he flashes his lifetime membership. I smile, happy to see him, and he nods politely as he walks over to the newer exhibits. He tries to appear interested, paces from piece to piece, but I know what he has come here to see. It is always the same thing. The spoons.

On the second floor of the museum, there is a small exhibit in the permanent collection consisting of more than four hundred spoons. They are simply presented, attached to glass-fronted corkboards like butterflies on display. Although some of the spoons seem quite old, genuine antiques, they are mostly your standard variety of silverware, all different patterns. They are ordinary enough to make you wonder why someone collected them, but there are so many that you understand that there is a very specific, very important reason that someone did it. But that person is dead, and the spoons are here, and the doctor stands in front of them, curious.

Though the doctor is old, I cannot help but be interested in him. He has silvery-white hair and a clean, handsome face. He walks confidently through the museum, his back straight. His smile touches something in me that has been dormant for quite some time. Am I a lonely old maid? No. On the road toward becoming a lonely old maid? Maybe so. Still, I am trying. But the doctor is preoccupied and does not notice my advances, however tentative they may be. On Wednesdays from noon until one, he cares about one thing, or one group of things. Those damn spoons.

∘∘
∘∘

When people call to ask about the museum exhibits, I tell them it is post-postmodern. Or premodern. "So," they say, "like um . . . conceptual art?" Yes, exactly. Exactly. They still don't come.

∘∘
∘∘

For the opening reception of the museum's new exhibit, I put out box wine, chessmen cookies, a carrot and celery platter with dip, and blocks of cheese. This is the standard MOW spread. Less would draw attention to the already shabby reception. More would make people think, "All this food . . . for this?" Maybe I'm only imagining this.

The exhibit consists of the letters of the alphabet cut out of magazines and books and newspapers by a now-deceased teenager from Hunstville, Alabama. The boy kept each letter, thousands and thousands of multicolored, multifont G's for instance, in thick album folders with plastic sleeves. When the time came for him to write something, say a note to a pen pal, he spelled out the text using the cutout letters, giving each note he wrote a ransom-letter quality. That alone would have earned him a place here at the MOW.

However, the museum places a great deal of emphasis on the emotional resonance of the work. The items being collected are heightened by the space they took up in that person's life, how much they relied on these objects. Therefore, when the boy spelled out his suicide note with some of the letters from his collection—*I don't think I belong here*—the museum had its next exhibit.

Of course, these are subconscious notions of the board of directors that I have noticed, not written parameters that they follow strictly. Also, it isn't as if the MOW goes after these pieces. The museum is contacted each time, the pieces donated in good faith that they will be exhibited and taken care of. So, when the parents of the boy contacted the board of directors, wanting only for the letters to be somewhere far from their home, the museum took them. It is an act of goodwill, preserving the things that others cannot or do not want to understand.

The reception is sparsely attended. The board of directors is here with their patient spouses. There are a few quiet, museum types who pore over the newspaper's arts section for some excuse to leave their apartments. And there are some college students who are here only for the box wine. The boy's parents aren't even here, could not bear to see their son's obsessive unhappiness displayed. I stay by the food. I've seen the exhibit many times over, getting it ready for the show. It was my idea to extend the exhibit the length of the wall, each letter shelved and lit individually. This way, each visitor can flip through the pages of all twenty-six of the folders, from *A* to *Z*. At the end of the alphabet is the suicide letter, framed in a simple metal rectangle. A little morbid, yes, but show me a museum that isn't.

The board of directors huddles around every album folder, flipping slowly through each page. They comment on the thorough care the boy took, the precision of the cutout letters, the angle of each positioned *B* in the folder. This is what they appreciate. They do not question the why, only the how. When they reach the end of the folders, they stare at the suicide note for a few seconds and then head back to the reception table for some more celery sticks.

What I think about when I stare at the alphabetized folders is how many letters it took, how many *D*'s and *O*'s and *R*'s it took before the boy realized they would never say the things he wanted them to. How many letters before he felt he had enough to spell the simple message he had been thinking of for months. I imagine him looking down at all of his albums of language and knowing not a single bit of it could help. So, he got rid of it the only way he saw fit. And this is where I find myself coming to terms with the piece, the feeling that the objects in your life begin to take over, fill up your life, and there is only so much you can take before you have to give it away, or leave it behind.

Once everyone has left, the doors locked, the lights dimmed, I walk past each exhibit, making sure everything is accounted for, that nothing has been misplaced. Each room that I walk out of, I flick the light switch and darkness trails behind me. I finish up at the new exhibit. I linger at the suicide note: *I don't think I belong here.* I turn off the final light and walk up the stairs to my room, which is the same way I left it, empty.

∷

On the phone, my mother says, "You don't care about anything, Janey. That's no way to live your life."

"I care about things, Mother, you know I do," I say. "You're just being mean."

"Well," she says, "you don't *want* anything."

"Maybe. I don't know."

"It's just as bad as not caring about anything, honey," she tells me. "You care and then you want and then you get and then you . . ."

"Then what?" I ask.

"Well, then you keep finding more things you care about and then you want those things and so you get them and you're life keeps expanding and getting richer. That's the way it works."

"And what do you want, Mother?"

"You know darn well what I want. I want you to be happy and find someone and get married and have kids and be fulfilled. And I want you to do it before I get too old and start getting senile and can't enjoy it."

"You aren't giving me much time then."

"Get out of that museum," she says, almost shouting.

⁰⁰

In the basement, searching for an older exhibit that has been in storage for the past year and is scheduled to be rotated into the museum, I find a small Styrofoam box. It is about the size of a shoe box, unlabeled, which is strange for this museum. I cut through the packing tape and inside is a small plastic bag holding six spoons. I immediately think of the doctor and try to imagine what these spoons might mean to him, the look on his face when he sees them. It is not a discovery on par with ancient ruins or dinosaur bones, but it is what one would call a foot in

the museum of whatnot   177

the door, or a twist of fate, or a snowball's chance in hell. Whatever it is, I am grateful.

I take out a piece of corkboard and cut it down to hold these six spoons. I attach each one, using a ruler to line them up. After that, I type up small labels and place them beside each new spoon. When this is finished, I place the entire project inside a glass frame and carry the frame upstairs, forgetting all about the old exhibit, understanding, for a brief second, the joy of possessing something, of putting meaning into an object.

○○
○○

In the mail, I receive a package from my ex-boyfriend. It is a copy of his novel, which is called *In Flight, at Rest,* and the cover is a painting of a man holding on to the legs of a flying bird. Inside the book, on the title page, is a handwritten note, which reads: *Did you ever believe I would finish? Probably not, but I did. Enjoy.* Over the weekend, I read the entire book and am pleased to admit that it is good, better than I had expected. For some reason, this admission makes me feel mature, as if I do not begrudge the things I have left behind. I take an X-Acto blade and carefully cut out the title page, with his note, and throw it away. Then I walk three blocks to the library, where I donate the book.

○○
○○

When the doctor arrives on the following Wednesday, I wave to him and try to explain about the new spoons but I cannot think of what to say, feel afraid for some reason that he won't care. While he stands patiently, waiting for me to speak, he seems so kind, the way his head tilts slightly as if waiting for a patient to explain a strange symptom, one he has undoubtedly encountered before. I shake my head and look down at the desk, and he continues walking, the metal of his stethoscope knocking faintly against the buttons of his shirt.

It is not long before he is back at my desk, face-to-face with me. He opens his mouth, but he doesn't say anything, his eyes still on me. He motions toward the stairs, gestures for me to come with him and I step out from behind the counter. We walk, slowly, up the stairs to the far corner of the east room, where there are six more spoons than the week before.

We stand there, still silent, and I watch him out of the corner of my eye, the amazed way that he regards these spoons, and I feel something light travel up my spine. "I found them," I finally say. "I just found them in the basement, in an unlabeled box. They must have been misfiled and no one had thought to look." There is a long pause before he turns to me, points toward the spoons, and says, "This," another pause, "this is wonderful." And then he takes my hand, encloses it with both of his hands, which are as smooth as every doctor's I have ever known. It seems as if he is about to cry, he is so happy, and I'm am grateful for the mystery of why there are things you can give someone that will bring them joy, that perhaps there is this capability with all things. At just this moment, it makes me want to find something else, something equally wonderful, to keep his hands on mine.

Back at my desk, I sit in my chair, expecting him to leave now that his hour is up, but he lingers in front of me. "Janey?" he asks, and it takes me a second to realize that he knows this from the name tag that I wear.

"Yes, Doctor?" I reply.

"Calvin is fine." He laughs. "It would make me happier if you called me Calvin."

There is a pause and I wait for him to ask his original question, but he stares at me until, finally, I say, "Yes, Calvin?"

He begins. "This spoon business," he says, "seems odd, I'm sure. But I am very indebted to you, and it would please me very much if you allowed me to take you to dinner." I must look startled because before I can agree, he says, "Nothing untoward, I assure you. I would just like the chance to explain the spoon business and I don't know anyone else that might be remotely interested." I nod and he smiles back. "Friday?" he asks and I nod again, finding it, in the moment, so easy to be agreeable.

⁂

After work on Friday, as I dress for my dinner with the doctor, my mother makes her weekly call. I tell her that I can't talk long, that I am having dinner with someone.

"A date?" she asks.

"Dinner. Eating."

"With whom, may I ask? Are you at least eating with a man?"

"It's a man."

"And he does something, I'm assuming?"

"He's a doctor."

"This is good."

"You would like him," I say.

"I like him so far."

"He's just a little older than you," and then there is dead silence on the other end of the phone.

"I'm sure you find that hilarious," she says. "I'm sure you find that funny enough for the both of us," and then she hangs up.

⁂

It takes me a second to recognize the doctor, waiting for me at the entrance to the restaurant, without his white coat. He waves and I nod and we go in and sit down at a table. He asks me about the museum, how I ended up there, and I tell him the story: the ad, the interviews, the job offer. It is boring even to me, but he listens and smiles. He tells me about himself. He has lived here since birth, has left only for school, and still practices general medicine at the hospital. His wife died six years ago and he has since lived alone. He has two children and three grandchildren. He has no "doctor hobbies" as he calls them, no sailing or mountaineering or fine wine interests. He shoots free throws every afternoon at the YMCA and once a month plays in a pickup game, which is all his body can take. He likes archival country music and poorly written detective novels. And while none of these things exactly endear him to me or provide a common interest, the fact that there is not one specific thing that occupies his life makes me happy.

And now, after dinner, coffee on the way, he tells me about the spoons, which he continues to call the spoon business. "No matter what I say, I doubt it will make you think it was worth all the time I spent staring at those things," he tells me, but I tell him that I'd like to try.

"Well, those spoons belonged to my father. I had no idea that he collected spoons until he died and left his belongings to me. I didn't know much of my father, actually, because he left my mother when I was very young, five or six years old. I didn't mind at the time, or now; he was very cruel when I knew him. My mother remarried and I took that man's name and I didn't see my father again until ten years ago. He was sick and alone and so my wife and I took him in. Even then, we rarely spoke, and he died less than a year later. Anyway, that's the background.

He didn't have much for me to inherit but he had specific instructions to donate the spoons to the museum, which makes me think he came back here for the museum and not for me. I started to visit the exhibit every now and again. And eventually, what came to take up most of my interest was that he had so many spoons, and he wasn't choosy about selecting them, but he did not have a spoon from the set we had when I was a young child. He didn't take one and it made me inescapably sad for some reason, that he left my mother and me and wouldn't even take one of our spoons with him. It seemed like he had done it on purpose, just another way to be cruel to us. And then you found those spoons and, of course, one was from the set from my childhood."

"And that makes you happy?" I ask him.

"I don't know what it makes me feel. It makes me feel . . . complete maybe. There was something that bothered me and now it doesn't and I can move on. I don't even feel like he loved us; that's not it. I just feel like he didn't hate us enough to disdain one of our spoons. Good God, he was a son of a bitch, but he kept something of ours for his entire life."

"Well, I'm glad I found it," I say.

"You could not be more glad than I am," he says.

He takes out a little box and slides it toward me. "Thank you," he says.

I push the box back toward him. "I can't take this," I tell him.

"You don't know what it is yet," he says, smiling.

"I can't take anything," I say.

"Well," he asks me, "can you open it?"

I lift the cover and there is a small, silver barrette. On the edge is a tiny black crow and its eye is made from the tiniest red ruby I have ever seen, like a pinprick of a jewel. "It's very beautiful," I tell him.

He nudges it closer to me. "I saw that you wear them a lot, and I found it yesterday at the antique shop. But you can't take it?" he says.

I place my hand over the box and look up at him. "Nothing else," I say.

"Not a single thing more," he says and lifts his hands off the table in surrender.

Back in my room, I take the box out of my purse and look around at the things that surround me. I try to imagine a spot where I can place the box and every possibility seems to draw too much attention to the object, make the rest of the room seem empty. I take the barrette out of the box and put it in the medicine cabinet, with my other barrettes. When I return to my room, I take the coins that are on top of my dresser and place them in the box. Usefulness is the key, finding ways to make things fit, but there is only so much that a person needs.

⁑

The next morning, just as the museum opens, the doctor appears with a little boy. I am wearing his barrette in my hair. He sees it and I feel a sharp rush of frustration, anticipating his mentioning it, but he does not say a thing. He only nudges the boy toward me and says, "This is my grandson, Henry, and I thought I could show him around." I tell him that is fine. "Would you care to walk with us?" he asks but I say that I must stay behind the desk in case other visitors arrive. We both smile at this and then I finally give in and lead them into the main room.

On rare occasions, teachers have brought their classes to the museum, so I have some experience with children. I know to steer them away from the pieces that require too much explanation, the kind that makes everyone confused or depressed.

Instead, I show Henry a row of jars filled with one man's lifetime accumulation of his toenail clippings, which is sufficiently gross to be engaging. Then I lead them over to the Cracker Jack display, which holds one man's entire collection of Cracker Jack toys, nearly eight thousand knickknacks, which was recently on loan to a toy museum in Michigan. The doctor looks at the exhibits with interest, as if this is the first time he has seen them, and perhaps it is, his preoccupation with the spoon business blinding him to the other pieces. While we stand behind the boy, staring at each exhibit, the doctor places his hand on the small of my back and I let him, because it is only his hand and I know he will need it soon.

When we are finished, and it does not take long, the doctor buys Henry a T-shirt, which is the first sale ever and even this makes me happy, getting rid of inventory. The doctor invites me to dinner again tonight, but I decline. "You need time to yourself," he says, nodding in an understanding manner that seems very much like a doctor. "I do," I say, though I am embarrassed to admit that I have no idea what that time will be spent doing. Dusting perhaps.

∷

Big news comes from the board of directors. William Saroyan, the famous writer, donated his works to a university in California. The one stipulation was that they would also oversee his collection of whatnot, which amounts to, among other things, boxes upon boxes of rocks and eleven garbage bags filled with rubber bands. The university, understandably, contacted the museum to learn of our interest. Interest was overwhelming.

"Just think," the head of the board of directors tells me, "one of the greatest creative minds of our times, and he collected all this wonderfully mundane bric-a-brac." To me, it just seems slightly embarrassing, that someone of his talent still had to squirrel away rubber bands. But it is a big deal and will probably result in news coverage and that, reminds the president, "will bring more collectors our way."

The shipment will arrive in a week, so it doesn't give me much time to prepare. I decide to leave the letter albums of the teenage boy in the main room and focus on the room beyond it, which is slightly larger and has better natural light. At night, I draw detailed maps of the room, trying my best to figure out how to creatively display eleven thousand paper clips. It makes me wonder if one's obsessions are like goldfish, growing only as large as the constraints will allow.

When Wednesday arrives, I forget about the doctor, and when he shows, I am in the basement, storing exhibits to make room for Saroyan's collection. When I ascend from the basement, he is waiting, his white coat and stethoscope calming me, reminding me of the time when he was near enough that I could see him but not close enough to accept his gifts. "Did you look at the spoons?" I ask him and he stares up at the ceiling and then leans over my desk. "I did but they did not hold my interest. In fact, I do not really care about the spoons at all anymore and yet, here I am, in the museum, and I can't quite understand why." It has been three weeks since our dinner and though I am pleasant when he is around, I am also reticent to engage him, turning down requests for dinner, making myself scarce during his Wednesday visits. The fact is that he is charming and handsome and kind, but my room is very small. I am afraid that the space that I occupy, which has always felt comfortable, will become less so with someone next to me. He does not get the hint.

"Dinner?" he asks hopefully. I tell him how busy I am with the Saroyan exhibit. "You do find the spoon business distressing, don't you?" he says. I shake my head.

"I'm just," I say, "really busy."

He looks at me as if he has just discovered something potentially troubling during an examination, a new mole or a rapid loss of motor skills. "I am old enough to have heard that a few times and I know enough to salvage what dignity I have left." He turns to leave and then stops just before he steps out the door. "Though that dinner invitation is good any day of the week. There, now I've gotten rid of all my dignity," he says, as he walks outside. "I don't like to hang on to things either."

∷

"You seeing the doctor still?" my mother asks me on the phone.

"No," I say.

"Well, that is too bad."

"I thought he was too old for your tastes."

"He is too old," she says. "That's a fact. But he's a doctor. And he got you to leave that damn museum. He's okay by me."

"Well, I am not seeing him."

"You said that already. And, if you recall, I said that was too bad."

∷

It is nearly closing time the following Wednesday when I realize that the doctor has not shown up. The first thing that I feel when I realize this is disappointment, though I do not want to admit it. While I may decline his dinner invitations, I like the feeling I have when he is on the second floor and I am at my desk and things seem not quite so empty. But he does not show, and I keep trying to figure out a way to display the Saroyan junk. I slipped up on the phone with one of the board members a few days ago and called it just that, "the Saroyan junk." He coughed softly and then said, "Junk isn't a synonym for whatnot. A trifle, a curio, perhaps even a gewgaw, but it isn't junk." I corrected myself immediately. There was a pause before he asked, "You haven't been calling it junk to the visitors have you?" When I assured him that I used the correct terminology in front of museum visitors, he sighed and then said, "Because calling it junk could significantly lower someone's estimation of our knickknacks."

⁑

A week later, the room is still filled with boxes of rocks, bags of rubber bands, paper clips in various bent stages, and enough aluminum foil to wallpaper the museum. But it is not displayed, merely sitting in the room while I try to figure out, still, how to arrange it in less than two days. I am having great difficulty seeing this as anything other than "Saroyan's junk" and that is a problem. The other exhibits, as strange as they might be, revealed something more, provided at least some aesthetic reward, however small. As a curator, it is hard to be excited about this exhibit, but I am trying. In the basement, I have built several clear boxes, each one as large as a bathtub, to house all these items. Over each box, I have created small labels that merely read "ROCKS" or "RUBBER BANDS." It could work, but I still am not happy with it. I am not happy with much of anything at this point, and then the doctor appears, holding his lifetime membership, and though I am still unhappy, it is lessened a great deal upon seeing him walk into the room, look around, and say,

"You're working so hard that you can't have dinner with me and this is all you've got?"

I am slightly flustered to see him and start moving a garbage bag of rubber bands toward the center of the room. "You're wearing the barrette," he says, and when I touch my hair, I realize that he is right.

"You didn't come last week," I tell him. "I wondered if you were going to show up today."

He picks up a handful of paper clips and shakes them around in his fist. "Elderly patient of mine slipped in the shower," he says. "I didn't think I could tell her that I couldn't see her because I had to go flirt with some woman who's been ignoring me. They'd rescind my license."

I set up two chairs and we sit beside each other, surrounded by the Saroyan collection, and he listens as I tell him about my problems with the exhibit.

"It's stupid," I say. "I know I should just arrange it and be done with it, but I don't like it. It's just junk."

"Everything is junk at some point," he says. "Museums are filled with the junk of previous civilizations, right?"

"I suppose. Maybe that's the problem. I just don't understand it. I don't know why people keep all of these things. I feel like something is faulty in my makeup."

"You still have the barrette."

"It's been only a few weeks," I tell him. "It could go at any time."

"But you could keep it forever. And I could give you something else, and you could keep that. And I could keep giving you things until you had boxes full of all of this stuff."

"But why would I keep it all?"

"Because I gave them to you, since I like you very much. And because you like me. And because it makes you happy to see something and think of me."

"You like me only because I found those spoons."

"I didn't always come to this damn place every Wednesday. Those spoons were around before you worked here and I would come maybe once a month. I wouldn't look forward to it either. I didn't want to look at those spoons but I had to, and then you were behind the desk and it became a lot easier to show up. And now I wish we could spend more time together and enjoy each other's company."

"I don't know," I say. "It's complicated."

He takes a rubber band from the bag and pulls it back as far as he can, aims, and before I can react, the rubber band smacks me in the forehead, a sharp stinging, and my hand instantly goes to the spot where it hit. "Jesus," I say. "That really hurt." He just smiles, slowly reaches for another, and when I see his hand moving toward the bag, I run at him, shove both of my hands into the bag and come up with an overflowing amount of rubber bands. "I think maybe we shouldn't get carried away with this," he says, but I am already shooting a rubber band at him. It hits him in the neck and he shouts, "Jesus. That does really—" and then another one hits him in the chin. For the next few minutes, rubber bands shoot across the space and once we are finished, a truce, I look at the floor of the room, rubber bands everywhere, and it looks perfect, the chaos of these mundane objects. I take another handful of rubber bands and toss them across the floor. "Are you okay?" the doctor asks, and I nod and then tell him to cover the floor in rubber bands, every inch of space. "This could work," I say. "This could be something good."

The doctor stays with me all night, arranging rocks and stringing together paper clips. He is calm and quiet as I direct his movements, but always smiling. When morning comes, we sit in the middle of the mess. Rocks are piled in strange pyramids and mounds, alien formations. Rubber bands, pulled tight, wait for the slightest touch to snap and recoil. Thousands of paper clips, melded together into unbroken chains, race back and forth along the walls, and aluminum foil carpets the floor, the ripples from each footstep bending the light into faint shimmers. Looking at all of these things together, it makes sense. There is so much stuff that it simply has exploded, covered the entire space. There is a point where the things you take on begin to overflow and then, finally, become interesting. You live with it, walk around it, and the randomness of it all becomes part of you. There is, I see, something pleasing about allowing something, however trivial, to fill up your life, to stop and look around at the space you inhabit and say, "I want this."

The doctor's hand rests on the space between my shoulder blades and I lean back against it. He kisses me, slow and tentative, and I let him. So he kisses me again, and I allow that one as well. When his movements suggest another, I accept it without reservation, happy at the prospect that there will be more.

worst-case scenario

I work for Worst-Case Scenario, Inc. I have a degree in Ca-
tastrophe from a small college in the Northeast, where I
learned all the ways that things fall apart. I am a field agent in
what could happen. I go to amusement parks and punch numbers into my computer and tell them how many people could
die on a ride, what we call *absolute disaster*.

I calculate what would happen if a city bus full of people
was taken hostage and then got stuck in a freak blizzard during
rush-hour traffic. We even have ways to determine how many
people would be killed if a disgruntled ex-employee came back
to take revenge on his former coworkers. I tell the businesses all
these horrible things that *could* happen and they pay me large
sums of money. They are usually very concerned when I leave,
very sad, but I cannot do anything for them. I can only tell them

how it might happen, not how to prevent it. They'd need another consulting firm for that.

°°
°°

I'm twenty-seven years old and I'm losing my hair. I wake up and there are hairs on my pillow, in the shower drain, in my comb, on the shoulders of my sweaters. I keep it all in Ziploc bags hidden under my bed, hoping that someday doctors will figure out a way to put it back. I am sometimes sick to my stomach when I think about it, the pink exposed skin on top of my head, like a baby's. That is why I have asked three women to marry me already. I need to find someone before the hair goes.

They all said no. Two of them thought I was joking and laughed. Stella, the one I'm seeing now, thought about it for a long time, lay back on the bed for thirty minutes, silent. Finally she said no. I figured she would. I don't think we are in love, although I think we could be if we tried a little harder. We say it though, because there is no harm in it. I won't hold it against her if she leaves.

Stella said she loved me one time and I asked her to qualify it. I asked her if she would love me if I lost a finger in a machine accident. Yes. I asked her if she would love me if I decided to become a bag boy at the Piggly Wiggly. Yes. I asked her if she would love me if I accidentally ran over her cat. Yes. I asked her if she would love me if I were bald. Pause. Big pause.

I asked her again. "Would you leave me if I went bald?" She didn't say anything, only bit her bottom lip, like the answer wanted to come out but she wouldn't let it. "Let's not think about those things," she said, like I had asked her about the ways we might die, something deep and unanswerable. I told her that I would love her if she were bald. "If I went bald," she said, "I

would become a nun and move to a convent in the mountains."
I asked her to marry me again and she said no.

I refuse to take any of the medicines for balding that are out there, Rogaine and Propecia and Tricomin. Those things aren't really proven yet, and they have side effects. I could have kidney failure from taking it, rare degenerative bone disorders. My head could cave in like a rotten jack-o'-lantern. Stella says I'm crazy, but I have the data to show her. I punched it all into my computer. She doesn't want to see it though. She keeps watching TV while I put more of my hair into plastic Baggies, like evidence from a crime scene.

••

Today I go to a house in the suburbs for a case analysis. A young woman with a baby in her arms opens the door. Her expression is serious but she gives me a slight smile and invites me in. Her name is Mina, and she asked our company to come over and figure out what could happen to their new baby in this house. She wanted to know if it was safe. She follows me around while I take pictures of every room, the staircase and hallways. I ask if I can get up into the attic and she pulls on a string that brings down a wood ladder and I climb up and take a picture. I get some air samples. I scan all the pictures into my computer. I ask this woman the prepared sheet of questions for a child-in-the-home case.

8. Do you and/or your spouse have an alcohol and/or drug problem?

97. Do you ever put your child down and then forget where he/she is for more than a few hours?

256. Have you ever dared your child to do something you would not normally do?

The survey is about three hundred questions, and most people answer honestly because they want to know how it will all turn out in the end.

When it's over, when I have all the information I need, I tell her that I will have a case of scenarios for her in a week. Mina thanks me and leads me back to the door, looking around at the walls of her house, wondering what dangers they hold. Her child is gurgling, making happy sounds. I smile at him, let him grab my hand and slobber on it. This seems like a good family, the kind of family I could love, and it makes me sad to know that the woman is going to have to hear about a lot of things that perhaps she didn't need to know. Her house is, without question, a house filled with theoretical tragedy, with possible sadness.

∞

Sometimes I watch Stella while she sleeps; I lean over her face and see how calm she looks, how perfectly peaceful. She is beautiful, probably too beautiful for someone like me, even now while I have all my hair. Sometimes, I trace my finger over her skin, starting at her neck and moving down to her stomach, the movement smooth across her body. She doesn't ever wake up. She sleeps the sleep of someone confident she will rise in the morning, which is nice. I like being around someone so happy, so quick to believe that the universe holds some kind of order and reason. She makes me forget myself, makes me feel like everything will work out fine. With her I believe implausible things. That we could eventually become the two people we want to be, in love and happy.

I watch her sleeping, the way a smile will pass over her face, surface from the subconscious of her dreams and out of her body like a breath. I watch it and think to myself, "What is she smiling about?" And I worry that it is not me she is thinking of. I gently poke her side with my finger, pinch her cheeks until she wakes, groggy and unaware. I ask her, "Are you going to leave me?" She will sit there for a few seconds, trying to become fully awake before she answers. Her face looks like she is concentrating, but then she always falls back to sleep without saying anything.

○○
○○

Before Worst-Case Scenario, Inc., I spent two years interning at a government-funded project called the Pangaea Project, where we tried to figure out what the United States would look like in one hundred, five hundred, and a thousand years. We had to follow weather patterns, fault lines, and environmental hazards in order to figure out what parts of the country would erode into nothing and what would break apart and fall into the ocean.

What we decided was that the continent would not change much in a hundred years. However, after that, all bets were off. Our graphs showed the West Coast entirely gone, broken off in random patterns and drifting out to the ocean like ice floes. We saw the South ruined by floods, the Mississippi River bursting in hundreds of directions like the branches of a tree, forming sub–Mississippi Rivers that tear jagged lines through the South like a hundred Sherman's marches. The Northeast frozen into wasteland. The country broken and ragged, only a remnant of what it used to be.

We wanted to get more funding to see how much further we could analyze, perhaps try to predict Armageddon, but the government got too depressed by the findings. They pulled the plug on the project. It still irks me sometimes that we never got to find out just how bad it was going to get.

○○
○○

Stella and I go see a baseball game, sit high in the center field stands. I wear a baseball cap to cover up the places where I am not yet balding, but probably will be soon. In the fifth inning, Stella asks me for the worst-case scenario. I don't have my computer but I don't need it. I watch for a few seconds, though she knows I have been keeping track for the entire game. Finally, I tell her.

The player at bat hits a home run, a mighty blast that leaves the stadium and crashes through the windshield of a car driving on the street, killing the driver on impact and leaving the car to jump the median and smash headfirst into the oncoming traffic, causing a massive pileup. A truck carrying hazardous materials catches on fire in the resulting pileup and explodes, which triggers a chain reaction of exploding cars that stretches for fifty yards in either direction. The noise of the explosions causes fans at the baseball game to run to the outfield bleachers to watch the commotion, resulting in several people being trampled in the stampede, some killed. One onlooker leans over too far and falls over the back wall of the stadium, landing on, and crushing, a small dog on the sidewalk below. The home team loses.

The player at bat swings at a curve ball in the dirt and strikes out. Stella looks over at me and asks, "What is that, then?" I tell her it is danger narrowly averted, a reprieve.

○○
○○

The following week, I go back to the Mina's house to give her the results. I go over the scenarios slowly, using computer-animated mock-ups for emphasis. One shows the mother dropping a glass jar of preserves on the floor of the kitchen. Her broom doesn't find all the pieces of glass and when her child crawls by, four days later, he presses his hand into a stray shard and cuts himself. The cut becomes gangrenous and the arm has to be amputated.

I can tell she is upset, trying not to cry. I feel the urge to touch her, to give her some kind of comfort, but I just keep looking down at the data. I realize how much I hate this part of the job, making people understand that the world is just one gigantic possibility. Things can happen that we are barely able to comprehend, and even less able to prevent. After I have shown the woman all the worst possible cases, I leave her the stack of data. She thanks me and holds her baby close to her body as I walk out the door and into the open air.

∘∘

Stella tells me that she wants to start a new company, called Look on the Bright Side, which will go to each business immediately after Worst-Case Scenario, Inc., and show them all the good things that could happen, all the perfect moments that they never dreamed possible. She would show diagrams where vast reservoirs of gold are found right underneath the business's building, safety records that go unsurpassed for years to come, and satisfied, loyal workers who donate parts of their own salary to keep the company going.

And she is right. These things could just as easily happen, but I tell her that no one will hire her. While people hope the good things will happen, they expect the bad things. Good things only make people nervous, like the calm before a storm.

∘∘

Some of the journals I've been reading say that washing your hair regularly will help prevent balding, that oils and dirt cause hair to fall out faster. So I start washing my hair twice a day with deep-cleaning shampoos. My hands are like prunes now, white at the fingertips. Stella wonders aloud if perhaps overwashing your hair can cause you to bald faster, the constant irritation of the shampoo, always touching your scalp. I don't know if she says these things on purpose, these hints toward failure. I go back to washing just once a day.

∷

Filling out reports at my desk a few weeks later, I get a call from Mina, the woman with the baby boy. She tells me that she can't sleep anymore, that she has terrible dreams of computer-animated figures falling down steps and being crushed by garage doors. I tell her that I'm sorry, but she wanted to know, most likely needed to know. Nonetheless, I also realize that what she really wanted was to know the worst and for it to not be that bad. But it never works that way. You will always get the worst; the unhappiest events will find you.

∷

In the dark while I talk to Stella in her sleep, I ask her, my lips brushing against her ear, "Are you going to leave me?" I lean over her face, my ear to her mouth like I am checking for signs of life. It may just be mumbling, perhaps only a sigh, a breath, but I want an answer. I fall asleep like that, my chin on her chest, my ear against her lips.

∷

On one job at a sausage factory, the owner became irate when I gave him my results: the computer figure falling into the grinder unbeknownst to any around him, the figure's children eating the sausage a week later, unaware that their father is in it. "This will never happen, never," he said, disgusted. "I paid you good money and you're giving me spook stories, doomsday predictions." He did not want to look at any of the rest of the data, tossed it into the garbage as I left.

Three weeks later, a plane dropped a frozen block of bathroom waste from its hold that didn't properly break up and crashed through the ceiling of that same man's office, killing him. It was actually in my data, scenario number twelve. For weeks the people at work called me Nostradamus, said I was so good that I could predict the future, but I knew it was just the law of averages. Something will happen sometime. You just have to wait for it.

⁙

I make a pillow with my hair. I empty all the Baggies into a pile on the floor, pull cotton from a hollowed-out pillow, and replace the stuffing with my own hair. It is a small pillow, like something you would place a diamond ring on at a wedding or hide a tooth under. It is heart-shaped and pink, something Stella will like. Once it is filled to bursting with my hair, I sew it back together, toss it in the air, and feel the weight of my unhappiness. I am surprised by how light it is.

I leave the pillow on my bed and when Stella comes in to go to sleep, she picks it up. I tell her it is for her. A gift. She is happy, thanks me, and squeezes it in her hands. That night she sleeps with it like a stuffed animal held tight in her arms. I watch her face, her smile. I think maybe this time it is about me.

⁙

Mina shows up at work. She asks if I can take a break and get some coffee with her. I tell her okay and quickly turn off my computer before she can see some of the mock-ups I'm doing for a fireworks warehouse. Bright colors and burned human flesh, beautiful and horrible all at once.

We sit down in the corner of a diner down the street, sip our coffee silently for a few minutes. She looks tired. It's easy enough to spot the signs around her eyes and mouth. But she is still very pretty, with shiny black hair that hangs down past her shoulders.

She tells me that she loves her child. She talks about the fertility drugs, how she tried for three years before she finally had him. The absolute worst immediately comes to me, the statistics of side effects from these drugs, how they cause terrible heart problems for the women, sometimes strain the genes of the child, making it open to all kinds of sicknesses, but I keep it to myself. I feel bad that I always have to think like this. For once I would like to give someone reassurance.

"I showed my husband the animations you made and all of the data," she tells me. "He just laughed, said he could have figured most of it on his own, if he was that kind of person. He told me not to worry about it. And then he said that he wished he'd known what a basket case I was before he married me. And now, sometimes when he's asleep and I'm still awake, I stare at him. I want to punch him hard in the face, maybe bite his nose off. I want to create a disaster and say, '*See. I told you. See.*'" She is almost crying, and I reach over to touch her hand.

She pulls me across the counter, kisses me hard on the mouth. Our lips are smashed against each other's, slowly moving like we are trying to talk but can't pull away. She holds the back of my head, forces me close, closer, until we can no longer breathe and have to separate. We sit back in our seats and I look at the loose strands of my hair tangled in her fingers. We both feel awkward, keep looking at each other and then away. I try to imagine the two of us together, but it would never work. I don't even need to run the possibilities through a computer to know this. We would weigh each other down with our worry. "Do something," she says, "please help me," and I kiss her again, softer, even though I know she wants something else, something I do not have.

⁘

While we are getting ready for bed, I hear Stella sigh loudly, call out, "Oh, what did you do?" I walk out of the bathroom, tooth-brush still in my mouth, and I see the pillow, hair spilling out of the tiny tear in the fabric where I tried to sew it shut.

I walk over to her and tell her I'm sorry. I take the pillow from her and walk to the kitchen, like I'm going to throw it away. Instead, I take out a big Ziploc bag and slide the pillow in. I hide it in the pantry, behind the cases of soda.

That night I poke Stella in the ribs and wake her. "Are you going to leave me?" I ask again, and she rubs her eyes, stares ahead like always. I sit back, ready for her head to fall back to the pillow, but then she says something. "Maybe. Probably," and she falls back into a deep, unmoving sleep. I feel sick deep down in my stomach. I lean over and ask her to marry me, but she is already far, far away.

In the morning, Stella tells me she is leaving. "I am sadder than I was before I met you," she tells me as she fills a suitcase with her clothes. I tell her that I am happier than I was before I met her and she says, "Well, then you can see who's getting the short end of that stick," and then she is gone, forever.

I stand there in my pajamas and watch her leave, unable to think of any reason for her to stay. My head is aching, and

I yank at my hair, feel strands of it pull loose and fall to the floor. I sit down and think to myself that life can not get much worse.

It takes me less than five seconds to know this isn't true, isn't even close to being true. Before I have time to think about it, I imagine that the walls of my house are finally so weakened by the termites I hear at night that they cave in, that my entire house comes down on top of me. I imagine myself buried under two stories of all the things I own, my balding, pink head the only part that is exposed in the rubble. I imagine myself yelling for help, but no one can hear. *Don't leave me, don't leave me.* The words echo in my head. So, yes, it could be worse.

⠒

Late that night, I go to Mina's house. I sit in the car and watch figures move past the windows. I have an armful of flowers on the seat beside me, the *Don't Worry, Be Happy* bouquet from the florist downtown. It is filled with bright colors, including a single sunflower. On the card, I simply wrote, "Smile. Things work out sometimes." I want one person to be happy because of me; I want to be the bearer of good news for once in my life.

Finally, when I can't put it off any longer, I walk cautiously up to the house, trying to stay in the shadows. A dog is barking a few houses away. When I get to the front door, I prop the flowers against it and turn to leave. And then I see her through the window, sitting at a desk. I move a little closer to the window. Mina is looking at the data I gave her, flipping through it over and over. Before I can think, I knock softly on the window and she turns toward me. I wave and she waves back, unfazed by my presence outside her window in the middle of the night. I point toward the door and give her a thumbs-up sign, and then

I hear a voice, a man's voice, call out, "Get the hell away from my house you freak." He is talking about me, though I don't turn around to make sure. I just start running.

I can hear him behind me, gaining ground. I yell out, "Flower delivery," and jump in my car. Before I can pull the door closed, he yanks me out and hits me, once, in the face. I begin to realize that this scenario has all the necessary elements of reaching *absolute disaster.*

"You're the guy that gave my wife all the bullshit information," he says, "aren't you?" I nod and he kicks me a few times, tells me to stay away or he'll call the police. "I was just trying to help," I say, "trying to fix things." He laughs and then says, "You're making it worse. Get out of here." I crawl back into my car and start to drive away, looking to see if Mina is there, but I cannot see her. The lights are off inside the house and the flowers are still on the doorstep.

∷

At Worst Case Scenario, Inc., I wait to be fired. I'm sure that Mina's husband has called management and that soon I will be asked to leave. It is rule number two in the handbook: *Never form personal attachments to your client.* Rule number one, the only thing more important is: *Remember, it only gets worse.*

My left eye is swollen and purple from the punch. I put aside the work I'm supposed to be doing and type in some new data, figures for the animation program. I don't know exactly what will come of it, but the variables are quantifiable enough to give me some idea. And then Mike, one of the ecological guys a few offices over, says there is someone waiting for me. I touch my black eye and wince, try to figure out if I can get out of the building without being seen. But I am used to the worst, so I walk out of my office, down the hall, and there is Mina, the baby in her arms, waiting for me.

We walk back to my office and she sits down, still holding the baby close. I apologize for last night. She nods, though she will not look up at me.

"It was nice," she says, "what you did."

"It doesn't matter," I say.

"I know it doesn't, but it was still nice."

There seems to be nothing else to say and so we sit there and listen to the nonsensical sounds of the baby. Finally she says, "I wish you could show me how to accept it. You must know how to live with these things and I wish you would show me how." She is close to crying and I turn the computer screen toward her. I punch in a few more numbers and start the animation sequences. I walk around to where she is sitting and crouch down beside her, point to the screen.

The animations start slowly but it's easy to make out the basic figures in the mock-up, a mother and her child. We sit silently and watch as the animations reveal a child growing up healthy and strong, year by year summaries, making the animated mother relieved that the worst has passed, that she can enjoy her life again. It shows the boy at school, swimming in a pool, riding a bike, all safely. The final animation shows a family sitting on a porch, happy, thinking about nothing but the sun going down in the distance, the purples and reds that fill up the sky. As I watch this last scene, I think that maybe it will not help, that all Mina will see of the family and the sunset is the slow way the sun creeps behind the horizon, the darkness that the family fades into. I think maybe we are all past saving.

When it is over, before I can stand up again, I feel Mina's hand on my shoulder. She leans toward me and kisses me so softly it feels like nothing more than a breath. She brushes a strand of hair off of my face and I tell her, "I'm going bald." She looks closely at me, her dark brown eyes sizing up the probabilities. "Well, you have a nicely shaped skull," she says. "At least you have that." Then I hand her a stack of information, the rest of the scenarios that I drew up today, equations and probabilities and narrative hypotheticals that back up the images she has just seen.

She starts to go through the stack of papers, then stops, and slowly, cautiously, hands the baby to me. He feels awkward in my arms and I think of all the different ways I could drop this baby, headfirst or feetfirst and on and on. Mina begins to flip through the pages and I can see her smile. The baby begins to cry, which makes my heart stop for a second, and then I hold him closer. I try to comfort him, and I realize I don't know his name.

"What's his name?" I ask.

"Alex."

The baby is still crying, but I say to him, "It's okay, Alex. It's going to be fine. Everything is fine." And even though I know all the scenarios, all the possibilities that refute the things I tell this baby, I make myself believe that it is true.

acknowledgments

A BRIEF CATALOG OF GRATITUDE: VOLUME I

Thanks to the following:

Agent: First and foremost, Julie Barer, my favorite person in the world.

Editor: Lee Boudreaux, a better editor I could not imagine.

Family, Extended: The Wilson, Fuselier, Shirai, Baltz, Couch, and Warren families for their understanding, support, and, in large doses, love.

Family, Primary: Leigh Anne, my first reader, and Griff, my future reader.

Friends: Leah Stewart, Cecily Parks, Phil Stephens, Matt O'Keefe, Erin McGraw, Andrew Hudgins, Juliana Gray, Greg Williamson, Erica Dawson, Carrie Jerrell, Daniel Groves, Caki Wilkinson,

Isabel Galbraith, Daniel Anderson, Lisa McAllister, Marc Schultz, Sam Esquith, Annie McFadyen, Terrence McGovern, Bryan Smith, Lawrence Wood, Heiko Kalmbach, Randall Kenan, Steve Almond, Michael Griffith, Nicola Mason, Dan O'Brien, Kristine Robinson, Ellen Slezak, Michelle Brower, Lucy Corin, Dan Wickett, and many others.

Journals: The literary journals where these stories originally appeared and especially the editors: Brock Clarke, Don Lee, Jim Clark, Allison Seay, Kyle Minor, and Hannah Tinti, who improved the stories with their suggestions.

Patchett, Ann: Ann Patchett

Publisher: Everyone at Ecco, especially Abby Holstein, for their hard work and uncanny ability to keep me from looking like an idiot.

Residencies: The Kimmel-Harding Nelson Center for the Arts, The MacDowell Colony, and Yaddo for the invaluable gifts of time and space.

Teachers: The faculty at Vanderbilt University and the University of Florida, especially, and with an infinite amount of gratitude, Tony Earley and Colonel Padgett Powell.

Work: Wyatt Prunty and Cheri Peters at the Sewanee Writers' Conference and the faculty and staff at the University of the South.

Insights,
Interviews
& More ...

Meet Kevin Wilson

I STARTED WRITING STORIES because I was lonely. I wish that there were more artistic and noble reasons that I put pen to paper, but the truth of the matter is that I wanted people to kiss me and I had the unfounded notion that, if I wrote a good enough story, people would be compelled to make out with me. This was not a sound theory.

I signed up for a creative writing workshop in college; the first story I wrote was about a boy who was stuck in a tree and a hobo who taunted him from the ground. People, amazingly, were able to resist the urge to have sex with me. The second story I wrote was about a kid who has sex with his sister's stuffed animal. People were now actively avoiding me. I was lonelier than when I had started writing stories. Clearly, I had not thought this through.

Were my mechanics unsound? Had I not grasped the art of telling a story so complex and emotionally resonant that people could not help but love me? I did some research. I found the short list for *Granta*'s Best Young American Novelists. Fifty-two authors. I read at least one book by all of them. In this manner, I discovered the work of Sherman Alexie, Rick Bass, Antonya Nelson, Ann

Leigh Ann Couch

Patchett, Jill McCorkle, Michael Parker, Elizabeth McCracken, Tom Drury, Lorrie Moore, Brian Kitely, Joanna Scott, Randall Kenan, Jeffrey Eugenides, Edwidge Danticat, David Bowman, and Chang-Rae Lee, all writers that I imagined as movie stars or baseball players, signing autographs and cashing novelty-sized checks. I wanted to make out with all of them. I wanted them to want to make out with me. I wrote harder.

I wrote a terrible story about a group of teenagers who take animal tranquilizers. I wrote an even worse story about a Buddy Holly impersonator who gets mugged. I was eating nothing but candy bars and sleeping on the floor of my apartment. I bought novels and short story collections as if they were self-help books or how-to guides. If I wasn't reading, I was writing. If I wasn't writing, I was reading. If I wasn't doing either of these things, I was practicing kissing my reflection in the mirror. "This," I told myself, "is what writers do."

The professor in my creative writing class took an interest in my work. I told him that I wanted the stories to be so good that people would make out with me. He nodded. He asked why I was wearing a beeper. "My mother likes to keep track of me," I told him. He said that getting rid of the beeper would be even more effective than if I had written "A Good Man Is Hard to Find." Then he looked over my stories and told me why they weren't very good and how I could make them better. I got rid of the beeper. I wrote harder. ▶

> 66 I bought novels and short story collections as if they were self-help books or how-to guides. 99

Meet Kevin Wilson *(continued)*

Slowly, my stories got better. There were still no takers in the "Make Out with Kevin Wilson" sweepstakes, but I found that I did not care as much as before. I was writing stories that were slightly better than awful and I felt a happiness previously unknown to me. I concentrated on writing stories that were marginal and yet somewhat memorable. I read every literary journal I could find, attended bookstore readings, and pored over author interviews. I started sleeping in an actual bed. I went on a date that turned out to not actually be a date. I wrote a story about a person whose parents spontaneously combusted. It was not bad. It was kind of good. I felt like I might spontaneously combust.

This is how I came to writing. For people who love literature, it is probably not an uncommon story. I wrote draft after draft of bad stories until they became something readable. I read book after book by authors infinitely more talented than myself and tried to learn from them. The only strange detail was that, as I was writing and reading, I was saying to myself, "Kevin, this is going to get you laid." It did not. This was for the best.

I'm married now. I ask my wife if it was my stories that first made her want to kiss me. She says it was perhaps the second or third thing, and I'm happy with that answer. ◡

A Conversation with Kevin Wilson

Which of your characters do you find most compelling and why? Do you see yourself in any of them?

The easy answer is that these are all thinly veiled versions of myself and so I find each and every one of them very, very fascinating. The more complicated answer is that I write about a few themes—loneliness and family and love—and so aspects of my own nature are bound to show up in the characters that I create because these are issues that have affected me and shaped my worldview.

I find the narrator in "Grand Stand-In" to be pretty compelling, someone who has lived most of her life without the need for companionship and family, or at least has convinced herself that she doesn't need these things, and then, suddenly, thrusts herself into other people's lives in such an intimate way. There's a hidden desperation that sits beneath the formal decision on her part to take this job in order to make money.

Your stories seamlessly unite the real and the imagined, creating mini-universes in which nearly all of the rules of the real world apply—just some, it seems, have been a little bent. As you're writing how do you balance the real and the strange and keep your stories believable? Were there any characters who pushed at the boundaries of suspended disbelief, who ▶

66 The easy answer is that these [characters] are all thinly veiled versions of myself and so I find each and every one of them very, very fascinating. 99

5

A Conversation with Kevin Wilson (*continued*)

were a struggle to keep from getting too strange? Were there any stories in which you wanted to pull back from the strange? What do you think is the most imaginative story in your collection?

The story generally shows you how far you can take it. It starts to make funny sounds when you stretch the boundaries of suspended disbelief too far. In "The Choir Director Affair," because the initial shock of the baby's teeth is so disorienting, I tried not to push the character much further and risk the baby becoming less of a baby and more of a creature that resembles a baby. I still couldn't resist making the kid eat a Big Mac, however.

And, honestly, the world we live in is so bizarre, so alien to rules and logic, that it's not hard to create a strange circumstance and make it seem plausible. The real trick, something that I work hardest at accomplishing, is to embrace the ridiculous nature of the stories without making the concerns of the characters ridiculous. To me, this is key. Even if the object of affection is a weird, toothy baby, the character still feels a connection to this baby, and that's what's important and what powers the story.

Several of your protagonists are kids or young people who have yet to fully join the adult world. What is it about their youth that is important to your stories? Some of these underage heroes are just on the cusp of becoming adults and seem to be having trouble with that transition—see, for example, "Tunneling to the Center of the Earth" and "The Shooting Man." Others we meet have been or are being forced into a kind of premature adulthood by taking on a huge responsibility, as in "Birds in the House" and "Blowing Up on the Spot." Do the characters avoiding responsibility and those who have been forced to take it on share any qualities? How would you characterize Scotty and Wynn from "Mortal Kombat"— are they taking on a responsibility or avoiding one?

I wrote a lot of these stories in the period between youth and adulthood, so I'm sure it rubbed off onto the stories. And with youthful characters, there is the newness of experience that I find interesting. This is not the sixth or seventh relationship for Penny in "Go, Fight, Win"; this is her first love. It's more complicated and mystifying as a result. The kids in "Tunneling to the Center of the Earth" have never had a mortgage or worked a full-time job and so the prospect of an adult life is more bizarre to them than the idea of living underground. Without that naivety of youth, the characters' actions become a little more difficult to understand.

As for the connection between the adults who want to stay children and the children that are forced to be adults, they are all afraid of being left behind. In "Tunneling to the Center of the Earth," the kids don't know what to make of the adult world and so they cling to each other for reassurance in the face of that uncertainty. The narrator in "Birds in the House," having already lost his mother, becomes an adult in order to hold onto his father, to prevent the rest of his family from falling apart. The same holds for the narrator in "Blowing Up on the Spot," who is terrified, having lost his parents in such an unexpected manner, of being left alone, without his brother or his new love. These people either hide in the past or throw themselves into the present in order to stave off loneliness.

It's difficult to say whether Scotty and Wynn are taking on or avoiding responsibility, but I think a sixteen-year-old faced with this situation, one that they believe will define them for the rest of their lives, could be forgiven for trying to hide from the possible repercussions.

Stylistically, "The Dead Sister Handbook" stands out from every other story in the collection—what inspired this story? Why write it as a handbook?

The story originated with the phrase "love apples." A friend of mine had given me this strange, old cookbook called *Love Apples and Other Garden Sass*, and while the recipes were interesting from a historical standpoint, the real winners were these random bits of advice and non-linear family histories that were interspersed in the book. I liked how something ostensibly about cooking became weirder as it progressed, which is what I ended up trying to do with my story. There is the frame of a handbook that becomes ▶

A Conversation with Kevin Wilson *(continued)*

something else entirely, the individual story of a brother and sister. Of course, Ben Marcus and his collection *The Age of Wire and String* was helpful in terms of having a template that I could study, and Judy Budnitz wrote a story called "Scenes from the Fall Fashion Catalog" that I've come back to many times. "The Dead Sister Handbook" is ultimately something that I'm finding myself drawn to more and more, discovering ways to be experimental while not losing what I care most about, which is narrative.

In "Go, Fight, Win," Penny is significantly older than the boy. It keeps the two characters in limbo between a romantic relationship and a sibling-like relationship—why is this important to the story?

Without it, I'm not sure where the conflict would occur. Penny and the boy are sensitive, kind people who appreciate the uniqueness of the other and don't want to change those wonderful aspects. The only reason they have to hide is because people would freak out (understandably so, I might add) to see this sixteen-year-old girl and this little kid making out. If not for their age, it would be a story about an athlete and a basket case who find love, which is basically *The Breakfast Club*.

In "Grand Stand-In," "Tunneling to the Center of the Earth," and "Worst-Case Scenario," you have created characters who initially find happiness in odd pursuits, only to become ensnared in the complications of those pursuits and choose to abandon them. In turn, when you end these stories, you write out the possibility for the character to again become a stand-in grandmother or a tunneler or a Worst-Case Scenario consultant. Why must these characters move on? Why is that important to the ending of these stories?

In some ways, the characters have to move on to avoid going crazy or totally losing the qualities that redeem them. Speaking from personal experience, there's only so long you can live in an underground tunnel before you have to surface. There is sadness at having failed in some way, but there is at least the promise of something better to come.

Why is "The Choir Director Affair" written in the second person? Who are the protagonists and antagonists in this story?

For this story, I wanted to use the second person, a voice that I am fond of, because of the way in which the story was progressing according to the desires of the character instead of the narrator/ writer. So it seemed essential that the narrator would try to assert their authority in the story by talking directly to the character, who keeps hijacking the story to places that it should not go. The character may not hear the narrator but he is being addressed. Daniel Orozco has a wonderful story called "Orientation," and in that story the narrator speaks to a "you" who happens to be a person on his first day of work at this strange company. The narrator is merely telling him about the politics of the office. It allows the informal nature of "you" to become something natural to the story, as opposed to a gimmicky conceit that implicates the reader in ways that he or she might not wish to be implicated. In this way, it becomes less "second person" and more "first person addressing another character."

Defining the protagonist and antagonist depends on which person you ask, the narrator or the character.

With parents who spontaneously combust and babies with sharp teeth, the unexpected situations and unusual characters in Tunneling to the Center of the Earth *seem the fruit of imagination more than anything else. Still, did you do any research for your stories? What and who were the real people, events, and experiences that helped inspire these stories?*

I do as little research as I can get away with. It's a slippery slope for me. For the novel that I am currently writing, I've found it necessary to read a lot of articles about constructing and firing potato cannons. I've read so much about them that it's not even useful to the story anymore. Instead of writing, I'm punching ▶

potato-sized holes into sheets of wood from fifty yards away, and I've wasted a lot of time.

As for the stories, I feel that "Tunneling to the Center of the Earth" would have lost something essential if I'd spent two pages explaining exactly how they bolstered these tunnels. I genuinely feel that when you present something strange and perhaps not possible, if you don't blink, if you simply incorporate it into the story without making too much of a show about it, it will have a better chance of being accepted by the reader.

With "Blowing Up on the Spot," my knowledge of spontaneous human combustion came exclusively from reading comic books and the Time-Life series *Mysteries of the Unknown*, which is the greatest thing ever written. To do any more research seemed unnecessary.

What is your writing process like? Do you get an idea for a character first and build a story around him or her? Do you see a particular scene and write from there?

I usually start with an image or a line and work from that, building a story to support it. For "Birds in the House," I had an image of a group of men pushing objects around a large table with hair-dryers. After many, many drafts, I had the finished product. In "Blowing Up on the Spot," I had the image of Scrabble tiles falling from the sky. The resulting story was my attempt to make that initial image plausible and interesting. To use a terrible simile, I start with a single Christmas ornament and then construct the tree that will support that ornament. This is perhaps not a structurally sound way to build stories, but it works for me.

Which was your favorite story to write? Which finished story is your favorite? Why?

They were all a lot of fun to write, even when it was difficult to figure out exactly what I was doing. "Blowing Up on the Spot," because it is one of the first stories I ever wrote, was perhaps the most fun; I was discovering all the weird things that I could do to a story as I was writing it. It was terribly exciting to realize that I was making something that might not be awful.

My favorite story in the collection is "Worst-Case Scenario," in some ways because I feel such a connection to the narrator, but also because it was the first hopeful story I ever wrote. That's not to say that I want every story to end happily, and I think a lot of people would say that "Worst-Case Scenario" is not hopeful, because of the experiences that precede the final scene, but for me, I felt like the character has a good shot at happiness and it made writing the story worthwhile for me. I was so unhinged and depressed when writing it, but by the end, I felt like I had shown myself a way to keep from going crazy. Perhaps that's my intent with all these stories. ～

The Stories Behind the Stories

"Grand Stand-In"
George Saunders's "The 400-Pound CEO" from *CivilWarLand in Bad Decline*

"In the area of phone inquiries I'm also unsurpassed. When a client calls to ask how their release went, everyone in the office falls all over themselves transferring the call to me. I'm reassuring and joyful. I laugh until tears run down my face at the stories I make up regarding the wacky things their raccoon did upon gaining its freedom."

It's weird but it's your job. So it's not that weird.

In this story, like so many others by Saunders that deal with the workplace, I love the way in which something as bizarre as a raccoon disposal company becomes less so when seen through the eyes of someone who writes up the invoices.

"Blowing Up on the Spot"
Tobias Wolff's "In the Garden of the North American Martyrs" from *In the Garden of North American Martyrs*

"Silence rose up around her; just when she thought that she would go under and be lost in it she heard someone whistling in the hallway outside, trilling the notes like a bird, like many birds."

I desperately wanted the ending of "Blowing Up on the Spot" to elicit the same kind of emotional resonance that I felt when I reached the end of Wolff's story, an incredible and completely earned resolution.

"The Dead Sister Handbook: A Guide for Sensitive Boys"
Allan Gurganus's "Breathing Room" from *White People*
"My ringleted brother is a small choice circle, like a target made of palest tissue paper, drawn drum-tight, and waiting."

Though I was equally inspired by the intensity of the relationship between the two brothers, one alive and one dead, in Chris Adrian's novel *Gob's Grief*, which is one of the most amazing books I've ever read, I'd always remembered this line from Gurganus's "Breathing Room." The sharpness of the observation, the inherent danger that the image suggests, reinforced the idea that siblings have the ability to see you in a way, real or imagined, that no one else can.

"Birds in the House"
Flannery O'Connor's "A Temple of the Holy Ghost" from *The Complete Stories*
"None of their ways were lost on the child."

Actually, this story began from a classmate, Katherine Landry, who wrote a piece that contained the repeating line, "The men in my family" throughout, which was hypnotic and wonderful to me and so I began to write hundreds of lines that began this way. At one point, I had the sentence, "The men in my family push planes made of balsa wood across a table with blow-dryers." From this, somehow, I got the opening of "Birds in the House": "The men in my family gather at Oak Hall this morning to make birds."

Flannery O'Connor's "A Temple of the Holy Ghost" inspired me when I began to flesh out the story. Knowing that I wanted to write from a child's perspective, I remembered the main character in O'Connor's story, named only "the child" and the ways in which she serves as an observer of the actions of her two older cousins. And the otherness of the child's Catholicism in the American South of the 1960's resonated with me when I dealt with one of the main aspects of my story, the half-Japanese makeup of the brothers in an otherwise traditional Southern family.

"Mortal Kombat"

Mary Gaitskill's "A Romantic Weekend" from *Bad Behavior*
   "She was terribly distressed. She wanted to throw her arms around him."

   When I read Mary Gaitskill's work, it helped me think about stories that I'd been wanting to write but felt unable to make the language fit the intensity of the characters' physical interactions. "A Romantic Weekend" is one of the best examples of the ways in which Gaitskill presents the awkwardness and confusion that come with sex, the way it defines and then redefines the people involved.

"Tunneling to the Center of the Earth"

John Updike's "The Hermit" from *The Music School*
   "There was no realm so small that it repelled distinction."

   I see a kinship between the three characters in "Tunneling to the Center of the Earth" and Stanley in "The Hermit," their desire to totally remove themselves from the known world. And while both stories present the impossibility of doing so, I wanted to find a way to pull the characters in "Tunneling" back into the real world without too much violence, to allow them to come back to what they had left with their innocence somewhat intact. This is in stark contrast to Updike's incredible story, which ends with a "thumping, a bumbling, a clumsy crashing clamor."

"The Shooting Man"

Steven Millhauser's "The Knife Thrower" from *The Knife Thrower*
   "Is it surprising we didn't know what to feel?"

   Why try to hide it? I read Millhauser's "The Knife Thrower" in college and immediately, perhaps that same day, tried to copy it. Millhauser had been a revelation for me, the first American writer I'd encountered to use fantastic elements in his fiction, something I had been trying, and failing, to do on my own. I took the essential elements of the story, the sideshow act and the shell-shocked audience, and then tried to turn the story into something more akin to pulp, like the 1950's horror and mystery comic books I'd read in high school, but there is no way to compare "The Shooting Man" to that incredible story by Millhauser.

"The Choir Director Affair (The Baby's Teeth)"
Aimee Bender's "What You Left in the Ditch" from *The Girl in the Flammable Skirt*
"Steven returned from the war without lips."

What I love about Bender's stories, and what I have tried to mimic in my own work, is the way in which she reveals the interesting element of the story so quickly, often in the first line ("Steven returned from the war without lips"; "My lover is experiencing reverse evolution"; "One week after his father died, my father woke up with a hole in his stomach") and then begins the difficult and thrilling work of creating a story that becomes so much more than the initial surprise. The depth of emotion in "What You Left in the Ditch" reminded me of the need, no matter how absurd the event, for the author to focus on the emotions of the characters who have found themselves, to their own great surprise, in such a strange predicament.

"Go, Fight, Win"
Padgett Powell's "Trick or Treat" from *Aliens of Affection*
"Her affair with this boy was as unknowable a thing as anything available to her in her life as it stood, and as it was ever likely to stand."

I imagined the boy in "Go, Fight, Win" to be the slower, sweeter cousin of Jimmy Teeth in "Trick or Treat." A better story about a supposedly mismatched couple you will not find.

"The Museum of Whatnot"
Lucy Corin's "Wizened" from *The Entire Predicament*
"It's true, I am wizened, sullen, frustrated, crotchety, but although the world generally annoys me, I have not lost interest in it."

While the narrator of "Wizened," like the narrator of "The Museum of Whatnot," is a solitary person, there are flashes where you can see the desire to connect with, or at least touch for a brief moment, the larger, outside world. I have read this story by Lucy Corin more than a dozen times and, with the depth of emotion on display and the unexpected ways the narrative unfolds, it never fails to astonish me. It is one of my all-time favorite works of short fiction.

"Worst-Case Scenario"
Sherwood Anderson's "Sophistication"
from *Winesburg, Ohio*

"In the mind of each was the same thought. 'I have come to this lonely place and here is this other,' was the substance of the thing felt."

Anderson's story is, to my mind, perfect. The way in which he connects two isolated people is amazing to me. So many of my stories are about lonely people who are trying desperately to find some kind of companionship, and "Sophistication" showed me how to bring these kinds of people together to become something stronger and more capable. In "Worst-Case Scenario," the narrator and Mina could not last much longer on their own, but by finding each other at just the right moment, there is the possibility for happiness. I feel the same way about "Sophistication," the way in which one character has the power "to make some minute readjustment of the machinery of [one's] life." One of the most hopeful and beautiful stories I've ever read. ⌘

Don't miss the next book by your favorite author. Sign up now for AuthorTracker by visiting www.AuthorTracker.com.